It Could Be Worse

by

August Sommers

Me. Well, most people calls me Marcus but my full name is Marcus Dinkins and   ever since I was little

growing up in Georgia I had a mind to travel and see the world so the first chance I got--I think I was

sixteen--I saved up a few coins I got from doing odd jobs around the place and jumped on the first thing

headed North.

Me and my best friend Henry Lucious come here together to New York City. We got us a one room flat

up in Harlem for three dollars a week so you know it wasn't much but for two younguns who ain't never

seen nothing but ol'man Miller's farm this seemed like heaven. But don't you know that just as soon as

we got situated Uncle Sam drafted us. Now Henry Lucious saw nothing wrong with us going overseas to

fight for the good ol' U.S. of A but me I was of a different perspective.

You see I had been listening to ol' man Miller for damn near all my life calling me boy and telling me to do this and to do that and I wasn't up for nobody else telling me what to do. But still Henry Lucious insisted that we had it better than most people around the world cause someone had fought for our freedom and liberty and it was our duty to make it so everybody could have it just as good as we had it. It was at these times when I'd just turn and look at Henry Lucious and shake my head. As good as we had it? I thought about Henry's words. 'It could be worse.' We was both working and there won't a week Ms. Kathryn didn't come a looking for us in her best Sunday church clothes and a bible in hand.

"Now Marcus when ya mama wrote me askin' for a place for you two boys I gladly said yes. I knowed right then and there that my dear friend Hattie Mae who I's known all my life wouldn't send me nobody that she didn't have the utmost faith in. Praise the Lord! So, I tried to lend a hand. The bible teaches us to treat our fellow man as you would like to be treated. And so I rented you two boys one of my better flats. And you been here long enough to know that you can't get a clean flat fo' no less than five dollars a week. I was trying to do Ms. Hattie Mae a favor but you two boys can't seem to be able to get together the three dollars that I'm asking. Now I ain't saying that you boys are like some of these ol' wild, crazy, Negroes out here but what I am saying is that I shouldn't have to come around here lookin' for you every time the rent is due. At three dollars a week it just don't seem right."

And for the first time I thought that Henry Lucious might be right and so I stuck out my chest and telled her in the most respectful of terms. I say.

"Ms. Kathryn you know if you is nothing else you would be correct and that's why me and Henry Lucious has decided that we's gonna join the war effort. I ain't rightly sure when we'll be leaving but that's our plan. I'm gonna personally make sure you get your rent 'cause you have truly been a good Christian lady helping us and all."

"Well, I'm glad to see you volunteering for the war effort," she said smiling at me.

What she didn't know was that me and Henry hadn't volunteered but had been drafted.

"You know I hear that a lot of our boys ain't volunteering and when they drafted they duckin' the draft and going into hidin'. What they don't realize is how good

America has been to us. Here I is the daughter of sharecroppers. Who would have thought that I could have been the landlord for three buildings up here in Harlem? I don't never have to work again and it gives me more time to serve the one responsible for all these blessings bestowed on me."

"I hears you Ms. Kathryn," I said not knowing what else to say. She was wrong about one thing though. I wasn't wild and crazy like those Negroes duckin' the draft but I agreed with them. I wasn't going nowhere to kill some one I didn't know for the same white folks that was trying to kill me everyday. Just didn't make me no sense.

"Like I sayed that's a good thing you and Henry are doing volunteering and giving back to the country that give you everything. You know a lot of people even in the church think I'm crazy when I sayed this but I'm going to tell you some words and I want you to dwell on 'em closely. In the bible iffen you read it as closely as I do you will see that there's a proper order for everything.

Have you ever noticed that whenever you tries to sit down and talk to Negroes about the problems we have as Negroes we tries to link everything back to slavery. That's just what we do. We makes excuses for everything. Ask a Negro why he ain't got no job

and he'll stare you straight in your eye and tell you that he been everywhere trying to find a job and there just ain't no job now that they got to pay a Negro a fair wage. But there

was no unemployment back in slavery. How is it that they always had something for him to do when the labor was cheap?

And you know what I tells them heathen Negroes?"

"No, what's that Ms. Kathryn?"

"I tell them they don't know how good they have it. Then if they have the time and let me quote them from the good book and I would read the passages referrin' to slavery where one man is suppose to serve another. It's written there plain as day. And what most a y'all niggas don't understand is that we were placed in bondage but if you have faith in the good Lord he will release you from this bondage in His own good time. And as you can see we is free which is a lot better than y'all runnin' around naked in the jungle all uncivilized with that voodoo and witchcraft in your head."

"I hear you," I muttered. I wanted to tell her how I really felt but we were two weeks late on the rent and I didn't want to test her Christianity right through here.

"You know if you boys had been up front with me and said you were having a hard time making the rent I could have probably lined up some odd jobs here and there to make up for it," she said winking at me as she stood and bent over to pick up her pocketbook. It was then that I understood just what type of odd jobs she had in store.

"What time is it anyway?"

"Six thirty ma'am."

"Well, let me see. I have to stop by the hospital and pay my regards to Ms. Shannon. She's having kidney stones removed and she should be getting out tomorrow so I've got to see her tonight or I'll never hear the end of it. Ms. White is a lot more serious. They're pretty sure she has the big 'C' so she'll be there for some time. I can visit her at a later date. So, that should give me an hour or so before I'll be home. Be there at seven thirty and don't be late. You have the address."

"Yes ma'am."

"And don't be late."

No, she hadn't just propositioned me. Or had she? No. Not Ms. Kathryn. She had to be at at least thirty-five maybe even forty. Me and Henry used to fantasize about her all the time. Ms. Kathy was thick as hell and fine. And the word was she didn't mess with no rag tag Negroes. No the word was that Ms. Kathy was waiting but we all would stand around signifyin' as to who was and who wasn't getting friendly with Ms. Kathy but one thing was for sure much as we wanted to it won't none of us.

Henry Lucious was head over heels in love, infatuated, in something with her but he and I were the only ones who knew it. Much as he tried to let her know it she pretended that she was unaware of his utter presence. He was already painfully shy so for him to even approach her was a major coup but she had dismissed him with a few kind

words and he never thought to approach her again. If I were to tell him what had just happened it would probably destroy him. And maybe, just maybe she had enough odd jobs that the rent wouldn't be a concern until something better came along.

There was a knock at the door of the tiny flat and then I heard the key turn. I loved my man Henry Lucious more than life itself. He was the closest thing to a brother to me even though I had three brothers of my own. That's how close me and him was. We did everything together. Sometimes it wasn't always good. Like the time we was coming home from over at Planter's Way back in Georgia. They had the prettiest little girls over on that there piece of property and they all seemed like they was our age. It won't but four or five miles and when we found out we was over there all the time.

One night me and Henry Lucious was coming from over Planter's Way and all of a sudden three or four white boys no older than us jumped out of the trees and started harassin' us. It was plain that they'd been drinking. Now Henry Lucious is like a slow burn. It takes a lot to make him lose it but when he does you don't want to be around. You can look at him and see he may not be the person you want to fuck with. Right now he stands six foot eight and about two ninety. And he's always been the same size. I remember he was about six foot twelve when he was nine. Seriously, though when he gets mad

Henry can cause some serious hurt and damage. I've seen it and these four skinny pecker woods decided they wanted to pick on me. They left Henry alone but that

didn't matter. Picking on me was the same as picking on him. Now at this time Henry was all caught up in the whole Bonnie & Clyde thing. He liked the dime store novels of

John Dillinger and Babyface Nelson and he bought this little broken down pistol that he used to oil, and polish and shine all the time. He used to carry it all the time and when we'd be alone he'd pretend he was Dillinger holding up a bank.

Well, anyway these crackers were talking about stringing me up and Henry Lucious lost it. He yelled telling them to stop. When they acted like they didn't hear he pulled that pistol from his waistband aimed it at the two closest to me and just kept pulling the trigger. When he finished there were two boys laying next to me. The other two were long gone. Me and Henry ain't never talked about that day. He stayed hid in a cave near where we used to go fishing for about three or four months 'til I had enough money for us to get outta there. That's when we came up North. We was inseparable then and we still inseparable. And all I can say is it could've been worse.

"Marcus. Is that you?"

"Yeah, man."

"Say, who you talking to?"

"I was just thinking out loud. Say man tell me this why do you knock at your own house before you open the door?"

"I ain't never had my own house. I guess I ain't use to having nothing where I didn't have to ask someone's permission. Whatcha have planned for tonight? DeAndre's having a card game and the Scott twins are supposed to there. Them girl's is thick as hell. I'm thinking about making one of them my wife. Just cain't make up my mind which one is all.   Gotta test them out thoroughly first," Henry laughed.

"You know you're crazy?"

"Yeah, yeah, yeah. You must have something kinda nice set up if you're passin' on the Scott twins. Just remember we have to be down at the recruiting office at nine a.m. and I wouldn't recommend showing up with a hangover. You never know what Uncle Sam may have up his sleeve. Can't never trust a cracker in power."

"I feel you. I should be home by eleven. I gotta handle some business. You know we're two weeks late on the rent?"

"Yeah, I know. Don't do nothin' stupid though. You can make the situation worse you know. You know the streets don't love nobody."

"I know man. See you later." I went to the door and smiled as I stepped out into the brisk November air. I pulled up my collar and I made my way the ten blocks up to the armory off of St. Nick's and into Sugar Hill where the wealthier Harlem Negroes stayed.

Knocking on the door of the hundred year old brownstone I was shocked when Ms. Kathryn opened the door looking like a Black Lauren Bacall.

"Oh Marcus. It is so very nice of you to come. If you will just have a seat in the sitting room."

I'd never heard of a sitting room but she led me a few steps and turned into a small room with two Queen Anne chairs and a parlor table. After several minutes I was quite aware of why they called this room the sitting room. There was absolutely nothing

to do but sit. There was much commotion and a great deal of scurrying in the house although from my vantage point I could see little. I sat in the chair and soon I felt myself dozing off.

"Marcus. I'd like to introduce you to a very good friend of mine. Sister Mary this is Marcus. Marcus. Sister Mary. Marcus, Sister Mary have an alternative for your rent problem. Sister Mary why don't you take Marcus upstairs and see if you can't work out some type of mutual agreement."

Sister Mary smiled.

"Oh, I'm sure Marcus and I will work out something," she said grabbing my hand and pulling me up the long spiral staircase.

My head was spinning. Had they lost their minds? What had Henry Lucious' slow ass just warned me about being careful out here in these streets? I still won't sure what Ms. Kathy or Sister Mary were up to but it smelled of no good. What I did know was that I was a big man--not quite as big as my boy Henry--but I could take care of myself. I followed her up the stairs to a beautiful bedroom that was larger than my whole

flat and I was suddenly at a loss for words. I didn't know what Sister Mary had to offer but this I did know. I was all ears. Back on ol' man Miller's place outside of Marietta we'd occasionally be asked to take something up to the big house and be invited in. Ol' man Miller didn't have no sitting room but in the hallway was a chair and some magazines. When I would look through them I saw great rooms full of fine furnishings

just like this. Only difference was that Negroes owned this and I was going to listen to whatever they had to say. After all, wasn't this the reason he and H. L. had made the journey North. Everyone spoke of opportunity and now he was seeing it firsthand.

"You like Marcus?"

I was suddenly released from my thoughts.

"I do. I ain't never seen no room so big. And to think Ms. Kathy owns all this."

Sister Mary smiled. She was a cute gal, not much older than I but you can tell that she was educated and she had that there sophistication the same as Ms. Kathy. And she spoke the king's English like a lot of colored folks in New York. A little on the plump side, the weight was in all the right places and she kinda reminded me of a colored Mae West with all the trimmings.

"Listen hon. Sister Kathy does own this but several sisters from the church are partners in it with her. I'm one of them and if you play your cards right you can join us in a limited partnership."

She stopped there. She had my attention now.

"We use this home as our place of business and serve the community from here. No one ever gets to come here but the few involved in our little enterprise so you should feel honored that Sister Kathy thinks enough of you to consider you for a position with us. Still, I can see why. You are one handsome devil."

"You still haven't told me what I would have to do."

Sister Mary laughed.

"Relax. It's up to me to make a recommendation once the evening's over as to whether I think you are right for us but for now let's just enjoy each other's company," she said pouring me a glass of some French champaign. Now I am not and have never been a drinker and after the second glass I was feeling a little tipsy when Sister Mary joined me on the love seat and began untying my tie and unbuttoning my shirt.

The rest of the night is a blur but I do remember Sister Mary screaming out on several occasions that night and someone coming to the room to ask for her to be quiet. She in turn had me take a pair of her stockings and use it as a gag. She could be still heard despite the gag but since she was a partial owner I figured little could be said to her.

When the evening was over she instructed me to get dressed and to have a seat on the love seat. I did as I was instructed and no sooner had I had a seat than the door opened again. Ms. Kathryn entered and took the seat next to me. My head was still spinning when I felt her hand touch the zipper of my pants. I immediately grew hard. After all she was what I'd initially come for.

"Down boy," she said smiling before getting up and pouring both of us a glass of champaign. "There will be plenty of time that. I have you penciled in for Sunday after

church. I spoke to your mother and she wanted to know if you had been attending church regularly. I told her I was your landlord not your minister but Hattie Mae begged me to take you under my wing and have you attend church so you will pick me up at nine thirty a.m. and we will attend church together and give the sisters something to gawk at. This is what white folks call good marketing. I parade you around church for a couple of weeks to get 'em all talking then we let 'em know that for a small price they too can have their very own boy toy should you agree to accept."

"So, that's what you called me here to talk about? You want me to pleasure those old spinsters in the church that cain't get no man."

"I wouldn't actually phrase it like that. We have a lot of good Christian women who were educated at the best schools and who are outstanding members of the Harlem community. They can't be seen in bars and nightclubs and just anywhere trying to find a man to get some lovin'. Understand that because these are Christian women they are not above having needs. You fulfill their needs discreetly and you will never have to worry about money again. We will have a woman to shadow you and teach you about class and refinement. It's sort of like our own finishing school. And once we're finished grooming you you'll be ready to take on any woman in New York City."

"And if I should choose not to take part? Then what?"

"Then I'd call you a fool. You'd still owe the rent and I'd say you're passing up a great opportunity to improve yourself and I'd hate to report back to Hattie Mae and have to tell her how you passed up on a great opportunity.

I think you'll be great in this role though. Sister Mary went on-and-on about you. She told me you were the best she's ever had. She even told me to hire you on the spot but from what I understand she's crazy about you anyway so I think a second opinion may be in order," she said winking at me.

"So, am I to assume that I will see you on Sunday morning or not?"

"I don't know, Ms. Kathryn. I really don't know."

"Well, you have a couple of days to decide. Here this should help," she said handing me a twenty dollar bill.

"What's this?" I said taking the twenty.

"Just a little something Sister Mary left you as a tip. Oh, and by the way she paid your rent."

"Oh," was the best I could manage. The job wasn't bad at all and the tip alone equaled a month of sweeping up fish heads in the Fulton Street Fish Market.

"So, will I see you on Sunday Marcus?" she said grabbing my hand and placing it on her breast. "I can only assure you that I will make sure that anytime that we match you up you will be properly suited with someone that you can appreciate and will help you expand your future. To me it's a win-win situation and if you agree I will grant you me

after church on Sunday at the same cost everyone else pays you. So, you see you can dream your fantasy and have it too."

"What time did you say?"

"Meet me here at nine-thirty a.m. sharp."

"I'll see you then," I said standing and shaking her hand before leaving. I lit my last cigarette and tossed the wrapper to the ground and wondered what I would do for cigarettes with payday not being for three or four days left and then I remembered the twenty in my pocket courtesy of Sister Mary and smiled. It really wasn't a bad gig when you really thought about it. It could be worse.

The next two days raced by and I rarely had thoughts of anything other than Sister Mary and Ms. Kathryn. What Ms. Kathryn didn't know was that it had been over a year since we left Marietta and in all that time I had not indulged in anything other than work and hustling to make ends meet. And that more than anything is why they had to come to the room and ask Sister Mary to quiet down but the mere thought of my landlord Ms. Kathryn was what I really desired.

And so despite the the bitter November cold I found myself at Ms. Kathryn's door promptly at nine fifteen. She seemed excited to see me.

"You know when I met you more than a year ago I said to myself, 'Kathryn you keep a close eye on that young man because that young man is gonna prove himself proud."

I didn't know what to say and simply held out my hand for her to take as I escorted her down the steps and to the waiting car. Once inside she turned to the window crossing her leg and exposing her chocolate thigh. Lord knows I thought I was going to lose it right there. Somehow we made it to church and although women approached throughout the service not one captured my attention the way Ms. Kathryn did. I was mesmerized by just the way she carried and commanded herself.

She then she made an announcement from the pulpit and introduced me to everyone as her cousin from Georgia who was single and any young lady interested in taking him out for a night on the town or helping him to get acquainted with the big city should give her a call.

And like that the service was over. We were soon back at the house in Sugar Hill. Only on this day the house was empty. Ms. Kathryn opened the front door and taking me by the hand led me in the same manner Sister Mary had up the stairs to the same bedroom. There was no champaign as Ms. Kathryn disrobed. I stood dumbfounded staring at her long, healthy body.

"Take off your clothes boy. Don't just stand there like you ain't never seen no naked woman before."

"Never see one quite like yours," I said grinning. And then I thought of my boy. What was it he used to say. 'It could be worse'.

We spent the afternoon and most of the early evening together. When it was over and we both lay there exhausted I was glad for two things. I was glad that my boy hadn't visited Ms. Kathryn. He would have been turned out and would have ended up her full-time flunky. But me I was different, more mature, always had been. The first chance I had I was simply going to marry her. I lay there smiling quietly next to my Black goddess and wondered what was to transpire now. Turning to me a cigarette in hand she smiled and then said.

"I have a few errands to run but if you're not doing anything later I would like to see you. Is there any chance you can spare me a couple more hours?"

"Let me run home and check on everything. What time are we talking?"

Pulling a twenty out of her purse she handed it to me.

"How's eight sound?"

"Sounds good."

"Call me if anything comes up."

"Oh, and sweetie-pie..."

"Ma'am?"

"I understand why Sister Mary was screaming now."

"You didn't do too bad yourself."

"Oh are we bragging now?"

"Not at all. You were beautiful."

"Sister Mary didn't lie either. You are quite talented. So, talented in fact that if you'd prefer I can keep

you as my own and you wouldn't have to entertain all those other horny, holier than thou, church-going

sons of bitches. But that's totally up to you. If you need the money then I'd leave my options open.

When do you leave for the war?"

"Next month."

"So what do you have? About three weeks left?"

"Yes, ma'am."

"And then you'll be the one paying. No. You'd better indulge yourself while you can. You know you'll

have a position here when you get out."

I returned that night and it was almost as if we hadn't left. She screamed for half the night and I refused

to stop and awake from my dream. The next morning she gave me another twenty and a ten dollar tip.

In the last week I'd made close to a hundred dollars and had a ball. But all good things must come to an

end and after telling Mr. Goldstein I wouldn't be returning to the fish market I sat patiently awaiting to hear from Kathryn. I had last heard from her on Sunday and it was now Wednesday. And then as if she knew I was thinking about her the phone rang.

"Sweetiepie, it's seven-thirty. I know this is short notice but I thought you might want to pick up a few dollars. Can you be here by eight?"

"I'm on my way."

Arriving at the Sugar Hill residence I found the house as busy as the first time I visited. The sitting room was full of women but then everywhere I looked there were women.

"Don't sweat sweetheart. Most of these women are for some sort of church function that ends at eight. The house should be fairly empty then but step into my office I need to speak to you about something in the few minutes we have."

"What's up Kathryn?"

"The women in the sitting room are here for your services. Do you think it's possible you can service all eight of them this evening or would you like to try and do half and reschedule the other four?"

I was so shocked I had to sit back and smile.

"If it helps any you'd be doing your country a great service."

"And how's that?"

"These are the wives of war vets. Their husbands are over there fighting the Nazis and here they are so busy defending the home front and supporting the war effort that no one has thought to consider their needs. Well, that is up until now. But you know Sister Kathryn tries to look out for everybody. And with that I encourage you to do your part for the war effort and our country. Now how do you want them broken up or would you like to try and knock them all out today and sleep in tomorrow?"

I was still smiling.

"To be honest with you Kathryn. I was lying in my bed thinking about you wondering how I could tell you how I was feeling about you. I had no idea that this is what you had in mind."

"Listen boy. I'm in a service industry. I service people's needs. It's a simple exchange. I give them the required services in exchange for a price we've agreed upon. When I slept with you I paid you and there were were no strings attached. Pay for product. Did I not make that clear? Once or twice I thought of keeping you as my own but then I considered how I would feel when you left so although I indulged I had to keep everything in perspective, a business perspective. So, what I expect you to do at this juncture is to keep everything in perspective and tell me how you want to do these ladies?"

"So, that's all it was? Just business as usual?"

"Oh, come on Marcus. You know that's all it's about. Don't get all new now?"

"You're right. I'm sorry Kathryn. Schedule them over the next couple of days. Spread them out though if you can."

"Gotcha. How's three tonight sound?"

"That's fine."

"Okay. You can go ahead up to the room and I'll send Ms. Farley up first. She is kind of a free spirit so you may just want to let her have her way. She's somewhat outspoken so I don't think you'll have to take the initiative. Like I said just follow her

lead. Might want to take some of that anger you're feeling for me out on her pussy and get her out of the way in a few minutes.

Ms. Arthur and Ms. Frazier are my age and I figure they won't last long. It's been sometime since either of them have been intimate so it shouldn't take more than a couple of minutes. Once they climax once you're finished. They want more they pay more. Whatever you decide over the top is on you. If they want to give you a hundred bucks for the night save the room fee and take them home and keep the whole hundred. I'm telling you at least one of these ladies is going to want to spend the night with you sweetheart. And don't walk away discouraged. You know Ms. Kathryn is going to need a night in your company before you leave for the service. Now go ahead up and get comfortable so I can send Ms. Farley up. I'm pretty sure I gave you the worst to start you off but if you can get passed her the rest should be smooth sailing."

I stood and Kathryn gave me a hug, a pat on the back for good luck and a box of condoms.

Kathryn certainly was right about Ms. Farley. She was different, a free spirit that wanted nothing more than for me to watch her perform things I had never seen before.

The other two women were cool in comparison. I think I was in bed with Ms. Frazier for no more than two minutes and as soon as I put it in she came. I felt so bad for her that when she went to pick up her clothes I called her to me.

"I know the rules young man and I'm okay with that. You are something to see though. That in itself made it all worthwhile," she said.

I ignored her and pulled her back to bed where I made her take her time and paused when she was on the verge. A half an hour later Ms. Frazier stuffed a wad of money in my hand.

"I paid Kathryn earlier. This is for you. Do you understand?"

I nodded and thanked her.

"You'll be hearing from me. You can bet on that."

She was my last client and after showering and getting dressed I met Kathryn who was reading something in the sitting room.

"Ms. Frazier was certainly impressed with you. She wants you to come spend a couple of days with her. And she gave me this to insure that it comes to fruition."

I didn't know what fruition meant but when she showed me three hundred dollar bills and handed it to me less thirty dollars which she said was her finders fee I said little.

"Okay you have three tomorrow. One at one. One at three and the last one's at five. You know you could cancel that sixty dollars and just concern yourself with Ms. Farley."

"No. If we've already committed let's stick with the plan."

"I like that. That means you're thinking. You sure you can't get out of that Army engagement?"

"I don't think so. I go for my physical on Thursday."

"Well, with your permission let me see what I can do if you'd prefer to be in my employ or you can remain patriotic and get shot at for Army pay."

"See what you can do Kathryn."

"I will certainly do that. I have a couple of senators who owe me favors. I'm sure we can work something out. Are you tired sweetie?"

"I'm beat," I said.

"Damn shame. That was Ms. Farley. She wants to see you again tonight. She claims she wasn't finished with you and you never made her climax."

"How could I when all she wanted me to do was watch?" I said somewhat exasperated.

"I told you she was different. I'm going to reschedule her for seven a.m. tomorrow and I want you to take her crazy ass and fuck her like there ain't no tomorrow. I want you to send her crazy ass home sore and limping. Do you hear me?"

I heard her but was too tired to respond. I kept thinking about Ms. Frazier. She was an attractive woman not yet pushing forty whose husband had been killed in the war. She had just received the pay outs from his insurance policies but it helped little with the

grief she now suffered. And all that grief and passion was evident when the lights were off.

"Anyway, come on and jump in. I'll give you a ride home. If you hadn't been so tired I would have taken you home with me and kept you all night."

I started to speak.

"Shhh... Believe you me I will have your ass in the next couple of days. That I can promise you. Hell after listening to Ms. Frazier go on-and-on about how you moved the earth and the stars I thought about going upstairs and raping your fine ass."

"And what stopped you?"

"I want you well rested and only thinking of me when I have you."

"Schedule that." I said sliding in the car.

I had her drop me off by Small's Paradise about a block away from the flat just in case my boy Henry Lucious was hanging out in front of the building. Henry Lucious was nowhere in sight and I was glad for that. He was already suspicious and kept asking who the new chick was and why hadn't he gotten to meet her. One morning he came in when I was counting my money and just stopped and stared.

"I don't even want to know anymore. All I know is you quit your job. The fellows tell me they see you all hours of the day. But no one ever sees hair or hide of you at night. And here you are sitting here with more money than Fort Knox. I can't wait for Uncle Sam to scoop your ass up before you get your ass killed in these streets," Henry Lucious said before heading out the door to work.

Five minutes later and promptly at seven Ms. Farley knocked at the door.

"Come in," I said beckoning her to come in. "Kathryn tells me you weren't satisfied last night?"

Before she could answer I commanded her to take off her clothes/

"In the kitchen?"

"I do my best work in the kitchen," I said not looking up from my morning newspaper.

Once she had her skirt and panty hose off I stood up and bent her over the kitchen table and proceeded to long stroke her. I knew she was feeling me and before it was over I'm sure half of Harlem knew it as well but I didn't stop. I hit it until she begged me to stop. When she left she handed me forty dollars.

"Absolutely the best money I've spent in a long time. And if you don't have anything else planned for tonight I'd like to see you."

I thought about it. I could always use the money. How long had it been since I'd sent mama some money? But this woman who couldn't have been more than twenty-five and most men would see as attractive did little or nothing for me. And different was not the word. Her husband had only gone active a week and a half ago and here she was spending some soldier's hard earned money to have some man she hardly knew bend her over and plow her insides like he used to do the lower forty eight.

"Depends on what time I get off work tonight."

"Well take this twenty and do it to me one more time just in case I don't get to see you tonight."

"Save your money and just call Kathryn. She knows my schedule. I'll tell her to make sure she fits you in."

"You promise?"

"Cross my heart."

"I'll see you tonight then Marcus," she said leaning over and kissing me flush on the mouth.

At one I stopped by the office to check in on Kathryn and she promptly assigned me to a room at the top of the stairs. Once there she appeared with a bottle of cider.

"Marcus there's been an unexpected change."

"What's that Kat? Seems like every time I step through these doors there's an unexpected change."

"And you've profited from every one. Tell the truth."

"I have." I said smiling. "What's up?"

"I can't handle all the requests for your company. The women have certainly taken a fondness for you. And the words spreading."

I smiled. It could be worse.

"I have twenty-four women all requesting your services. And then we have nine of those who want a night. Lord knows I've stumbled on the goose that lays the golden egg," she said smiling at me. "Is there any way you can knock a few of these out today?"

"No. The three you have scheduled for today is more than enough. Oh, and I took care of Ms. Farley this morning. She's going to call you to schedule something for later today."

"And?"

"Please don't. I have a hard time with her. I cannot find anything attractive about her."

"Melissa is quite attractive."

"She does absolutely nothing for me."

"And what does?"

"Don't play with me Kathryn. You know exactly what gets it done for me."

Kathryn smiled and dropped her head.

"It's a mind set. Do you trust me sweetheart?"

"You know I do."

"Then leave eight 'til twelve open and I'm going to schedule Melissa for those hours. And I guarantee she'll pay for the entire night."

"No." I said adamantly.

"Do you trust me?"

"I think we just went through this."

"Then trust me. I'll be there every step of the way to help you get through this. What I need for you to do is to punish it when she gives it to you? Hit it hard and make her come three times in succession and she'll go running home with her tail between her legs. But don't worry I'll walk you through it step-by-step."

Before she could finish the phone rang.

"Speak of the devil. We were just talking about you Melissa. Of course it was all good but listen I was just taking a look at Marcus's itinerary and it looks like he's booked solid right until Uncle Sam takes our little play toy from us. He leaves next Thursday. And like I said he's booked right up until then. He has three appointments tonight. He should stand to clear somewhere in the neighborhood of two hundred dollars. What you'll give him two fifty. Yes, money talks but I can't let you kill my star. Besides these women were paying more because I was aiding. You know he's still in training. And you know I know how you are Melissa. I don't know if you'd be willing to pay for my services as well. Yes, he leaves next Thursday. Yes, I think he and I may well be able to squeeze you in but not for the night. How will eight 'til eleven suit you? It doesn't. Yes, that's a lot of money. I'll tell you what. Marcus and I will service your needs for three fifty tonight. It's the only time I can squeeze you in. I'll set that up with him. In the meantime let me go get ready for your pretty ass. Okay, see you 'round eight Missy."

I was still marveling at how well she manipulated people to do her bidding when she hung up.

"Why are you looking at me like that? I know Melissa. Her father's a white judge down in lower Manhattan and one of the people I called on to help me have your Army status changed. She's confused is all. She doesn't know if she's colored or white. Don't know if she likes women or men. I'm telling you. She's confused is all. But ol' girl is in daddy's pocket and believe me daddy's got some deep pockets. I'm telling you if we double team her ass she won't last more than a half an hour and will be calling back in an hour. She's a nympho and a freak but like I said we can have her in and out within the hour.

In the meantime I think your first appointment is waiting on you. She should be waiting out back in the guest house. Her name is Martha. Martha Davidson. I'd say Martha is about fifty but in great shape. We work out at the same gym. She just lost her husband overseas so she may just want to talk."

Up until this time Kathryn had been on point. But not this time.

I stepped into the servants quarter to a very handsome woman who's close cropped haircut, caramel complexion and keen features reminded me of Lena Horne. The similarities stopped there.

"Damn Negro my appointment was for one o'clock. It's one thirty. Some people have to work you know."

"I do apologize Ms. Davidson."

"You can apologize by taking care of your business." she said turning and bending over the twin bed.

"And here put this on me so no one hears me," she said handing me a red ball with two black adjustable straps to be put in her mouth to muffle her screams. Then turning her back towards me she bent over the bed.

"I paid Kathryn. She told me you had another client at three. I know the rules and once I have an orgasm it's time to go. That's why I'm so upset. I have money," she said pointing to the table in the middle of the room with at least two or three hundred in twenty dollar bills.

"I'm multi-orgasmic and as long as you keep me coming I'm a happy woman. I'm just hoping that you can pick up a few of those twenties before your next appointment."

"I'll do my best."

"Then come on."

"Where would you like me to start?"

"There's two holes available to you. Makes me no never mind as long as you give them both enough attention and don't worry about hurting me. In case you haven't noticed I'm a big girl and I can take everything you have to offer. Now strap my muzzle on although if the shit is good I really don't think that shit's gonna help. Come on baby boy. Do me."

An hour later, I watched as the tears rolled down her face and she begged me to stop.

"I miss him so much. He was a big man, bigger than you and he used to drill it. Whenever he'd stop I'd be sore for like four or five days but it was okay. I loved him that much. And as soon as I healed up I'd invite him back to enjoy me again and he did enjoy me. That man adored me. You took me back there today and I thank you. Keep the money. Kathryn has been bustin' her ass tryna keep you out the war. Hope it works out for you. That damn war killed my Bobby. You keep yourself safe you hear," she said pulling the door shut behind her.

By the time the week ended I had put a little over twelve hundred away and was exhausted. The day before I was scheduled to leave Kathryn called me. I met her an hour later at her house. She was excited and enthused.

"Sweetie. I think I may consider keeping you for my very own after all. You see Melissa's daddy came through. Here's your deferment," she said smiling as she handed me the letter. "All you do is present this to the people at the recruiting office when you go to take your physical. Once they let you go come on back to me."

We spent the better part of the day at her place and despite her having me sleep with different women it was nothing compared to being with her. She meant the world to me. That and the fact that she reshaped my life. She said that we were good for each other. I think she called it something like a symbiotic relationship where we needed each other. I didn't say much of nothing but I understood what she was saying. I was glad for all she'd done for me.

I got up the next morning and Henry Lucious was already ready to go. I washed and dressed quickly before putting the deferment letter in my pocket. I wasn't exactly sure how my boy would take it when

I told him that his woman had saved my ass by getting me a deferment. This after all, was my brother. He remained my oldest and dearest friend who had risked his life in Georgia trying to save mine. And now I had to betray him in the worst possible way.

I was sitting there thinking about all of this when he turned to me.

"Bro, I know you're scared but has there ever been a time when the good Lord has abandoned us. And as long as you have faith in Him no evil shall harm us. Besides you know I's got your back."

"Man I ain't thinking 'bout that. I'm just thinking about missing out on the Scott twins. If anyone should be worried it should be you."

"Oh yeah and why is that?"

"Because you make the biggest damn target. Just look around. Ain't a colored boy in this room half your size. They like monkeys and chimpanzees. Negro you like some kin to them gorillas. Is you a gorilla Henry Lucious?" I said doubling over in laughter.

"You didn't say that when them peckerwoods was about to string you up back in Georgia."

"You right," I said still laughing.

"Like I said I have faith in the good Lord so I know I'll be back in two years. I think the only thing I'm going to miss is Ms. Kathryn. There's just something about her that says she ain't as religious as she claims to be. You know what I mean?"

"I don't know her that well. Outside of paying her the rent once a month I hardly see the woman."

"Come on man. Say your goodbyes. Be two years before we step foot back on American soil."

And just like that I followed my boy up the steps and onto the bus. Three months later I found myself in some small town I couldn't pronounce in the south of Italy. When we left New York I must admit I was having a ball. Kathryn was showing me a different class of Black folks and I was enjoying every bit of it. I have asked myself a thousand times why I left since I've been here. I guess it's just my overwhelming sense of loyalty. Still, any way I look at it it was a bad choice.

I've tried to stay in touch with Kathryn as much as possible. We write to each other about once a week. She says she misses me and I can't tell if that's any different than when she tells me Melissa is always asking when I'm coming home. I wonder if her crazy ass has thought to ask when her own husband is coming home. And Ms. Frazier has a plane ticket and a place for me to stay when I returned home. It was nice to know but my only concern was Kathryn. I'd already written to her asking her to marry me but

she never did give an answer aside from 'we'll see'. So, I stopped writing and wishing on a dream and turned the page on that chapter of my life and to this day I have never mentioned Kathryn or any of what took place prior to our leaving New York.

Italy was okay. The natives were friendly and seem to take to us. We were an all Negro detachment responsible for distributing medical and food supplies. It was easy work and the government put a few sheckles in a Negro's pocket so it was okay. Every now and then they sent us to the front to kill Nazis. We handled our business and did America proud. Henry Lucious kept himself busy between work and volunteering at the local U.S.O. where they had dances for colored troops. I think I went to one. It wasn't my thing and like Melissa these white girls did nothing for me. Henry, on the other hand was like one big teddy bear to them Italian girls. They were crazy about him and even though I wasn't clockin' my boy I gotta admit he had a different Italian girl in the barracks every weekend.

One day me and Henry were just sitting around shootin' the breeze and I had to ask him.

"Henry tell me something. I want you to be honest and truthful though."

"Has I ever been any other way?"

"Then tell me this. Do you have any real feelings towards any of these women that you bring to the barracks on the weekends?"

Henry smiled that devilish grin of his and lit a cigarette before looking at me.

"I suppose I feel a certain kind of way about them. I mean I do like them. There is definitely an attraction."

"I guess what I'm trying to ask is if you feel anything like love or is this something you're doing just to kill time?"

"Come on bro. We don't even speak the same language. How could you possibly see anything else there other than a good time?"

"So, why do you do it?"

"Because I can. This ain't Georgia. If I were to do this in Marietta they'd be screaming strange fruit. You know I was thinking of staying right here after the war was over. First place I ever been where they give a colored boy like me some love and respect."

"You're serious aren't you?"

"Hell, yeah and I'll always have that thing in Georgia hanging over my head. One day I could be sitting in my rocker with my grand baby on my lap and them crackers could walk right on in and arrest me for murder. Ain't no statute of limitations on murder you know?"

"We don't even know if those boys died."

"And I don't need nobody to pop up and tell me that they didn't."

"I suppose you're right. It could be worse."

Henry Lucious was serious about remaining in Italy and I can still remember hugging my oldest and dearest friend goodbye and then before boarding the ship home.

Three weeks later I remember disembarking onto the island of Manhattan once more. It was spring and the city was bustling and even more alive than when I'd left. I'd written Kathryn a week before my arrival and she suggested that I stay with her. When I declined she asked if I was still interested in making some money. I had nothing else lined up so I graciously accepted my old job back but this time I wanted to invest my money so whether I was working or not it would still be making money for me. I picked this up from some of the Italians I had come across and it made good sense too. So, when Kathryn asked if i wanted to go to work my answer was yes.

"Then you can start tonight. You can stay with me until say mid-week. I'll pay you the same as always and then I'll give Ms. Frazier a call and tell her your ship is arriving on Wednesday. And you can spend the rest of the week with her. Now you tell me what colored boy fresh out of Uncle Sam's army is coming home to seven hundred dollars a week?"

Two years ago I was earning a hundred dollars a night. And that was okay two years ago. But my price has gone up to a hundred and fifty a night now.

"Run it by the ladies. I don't think they'll mind much and the sleeping arrangements are fine but I think I'd like to spend the first three or four days with Ms. Frazier and then the final three or four days with you."

"Ouch! You do know how to hurt a girl's feelings don't you?"

"This has nothing to do with feelings sweetheart. This is all about business. I'll talk to you tomorrow Kathryn."

I felt no animosity towards this woman. In fact, at this point I felt little or nothing towards her. She'd been my teacher in more ways than one and this was a lesson that I took to heart. Do not mix business and pleasure and never but never let your emotions come before your purse strings. And with that said I decided to move ahead with my plan.

That night, my first night in New York City I called Melissa Farley. She'd matured a lil and gained about twenty five or thirty pounds making her even less desirous than when I'd left. Still, I knew that if there was anyone that would go along and finance my little venture it would probably be Melissa. I could have asked Kathryn but she would have her hand out looking for apiece and as every budding entrepreneur knows you can't split the pie before there is a pie and if everything came from me why would I split it.

"My condolences Melissa. I heard your husband was killed in Normandy."

The thirtyish looking woman dropped her head.

"I am sorry but listen Kathryn wrote me telling me you asked about me. So, I made it a point to make sure you were the first person I called when I got home."

"And I'm certainly glad you did. You know I haven't been with anyone since you left. Now where can I take you for the evening?"

"That's just it. I don't want anything but a nice warm bed. I am absolutely exhausted."

"I remember begging to spend a night with you before you left and Kathryn had the hardest time trying to fit me in."

"And that's exactly why I don't want you to mention I'm here."

"That certainly won't be a problem. That just means more for me. Come on let's grab a cab. You can stay at my place if you like. Are your rates still the same?"

"No, but for you they are."

"Well, thank you sir and what do I owe this good fortune to?"

"You are going to help me set up my new business."

"Whatever you need Marcus but can we take care of some overdue business first?"

"Lead the way."

I tackled the business at hand quickly. Melissa admitted and I was shocked that she hadn't been sexed since I left and in the two or three minutes it took her to scream out two orgasms I knew she wasn't lying. She'd stopped by the bank that afternoon and given me the hundred in advance hoping I would stay and then given me a key to her luxury penthouse apartment. She was asleep five minutes later. I showered quickly and

headed uptown. I'd written to Ms. Tuesday Frazier on more than one occasion when I was overseas and detailed my plans. I also sent her every dollar I'd earned at home and overseas. A licensed real estate broker she'd manage to carve out a nice little empire for herself and she's pledged she would do the same for me. I wasn't exactly sure what the attraction was between the two. She was fifty and I was barely twenty one but we got along well in bed and out of bed. We talked and laughed about everything and she was the second person other than Kathryn that I sincerely felt had my welfare at heart. A couple of times we had talked into the wee hours of the morning and then made good love for all of fifteen minutes. The next morning when she gave me a hundred for the evening and I gave it back I thought I was back home with mama.

"Boy I know you enjoyed my company as much as I enjoyed yours but this is business, your business. Don't ever forget that or let feelings get in the way of your money. Think of that money as the plate in front of you at dinnertime. Would you just let someone come and take your plate away."

"I understand."

It was clear she was annoyed and from that day on she began teaching me about business and business management and it was not long before she and I discovered how Kathryn who I had trusted had been holding out on me and skimming off the top.

"Oh, Kathryn's a shrewd one alright. She gave me the whole spiel about how you were her own personal but that for three hundred she might be able to convince you to

spend a night with me. That means she got six hundred dollars from me for those two nights right before you left and you received how much?"

"A hundred and forty."

"You know if someone had done something like that to Kathryn she would have had their head on a platter still been screaming bloody murder."

I let it fester for those two years until Tuesday Frazier and I finally came up with an reasonable alternative. She would manage me in the same way in which she managed her real estate holdings. She would find me valuable piece of real estate which was at it's low but sure to appreciate. I could rent or opt to buy and use it for business as well as my home if I chose to.

But first and before business we would meet and become reacquainted. Despite the age difference she was perhaps the only woman of the women I'd met through Kathryn.

A big grin engulfed Tuesday's face when she me saw come into the tiny bar off of Columbus. We hugged.

"My God. You have really filled out. You really look good Marcus. I bet you can't keep the girl's off of you."

"There is one I surely wouldn't mind being on me now," I said taking in all of her fine brown frame."

"You want a drink?"

"No."

"Then come on. Let's go. I live right upstairs."

She'd torn most of my clothes off by the time the elevator stopped on the ninth floor.

"Negro. I've been waiting for this for two years. So, let me see some of your best work."

"Two years? Now that's what I call loyalty."

"Come here Marcus."

She was wonderful and if not for the age difference I think we would have made a good couple. Tuesday talked freely and laughed easily. She was a woman of a good deal of wealth who had recently widowed and now buried herself in her real estate career. Her success had obsessed and driven her. It was with the death of her husband that allowed her to blossom and reach her own potential. It was almost as if the shackles had been taken off and she was now free.

Now she was guiding me through the intricacies of the business world almost as if I were her protege. She had me continue with the finishing school that Kathryn had forced me to go to to improve my speech and overall education. It taught me how to dress in a more refined manner and helped to shape me into a broader, more well-rounded person. I knew I made her happy behind closed doors but I wasn't sure if I could hold a

candle to her in her circles so I thought I'd bide my time and absorb as much knowledge as possible while in her company.

"And I'd love to have your company on a full-time business for say six months. I could whip you into shape. We could go to the gym and work out together. Wouldn't do anything but improve your own profitability."

"Sounds too much like the army," I laughed. "But let me think about it. I'd really like something of this nature. You know I have never had a place of my own." I said smiling. The loft Tuesday lived in was gorgeous.

"There's one vacant right across the hall."

"And how much does one of these go for."

"What's it worth to you?"

"I would love it but this is way out of my league."

"Let me speak to the landlord," she said smiling.

"I should have known. You own the building," I grinned.

"Yes. I do."

"So, what would something like this cost me?"

"Tomorrow we talk business but tonight it's about you and me making each other feel good."

"Sounds good to me."

When I woke up the next morning Tuesday was already up and dressed. I have to admit the navy blue suit she wore was a turn on and when she bent over to kiss me I pulled her back into the bed.

"Sir I just ironed my clothes."

Ignoring her I unzipped her skirt despite her feeble attempts to hold on to her skirt.

"Sir we have an appointment at ten and I have two other places to show you."

"Do you not know how I missed you?"

"I'm beginning to see but we have to take care of business first."

"Not after last night and not having anything but a picture of you for two years. Sorry but business can wait until I have my fill of you."

"Be careful but I'm detecting some feelings starting to come into play."

"And?"

"I'm okay with things just the way they are now. I don't let the two cross paths."

"So, you're telling me that you have no feelings towards me whatsoever?"

"Didn't say that. What I am saying is that I can put my feelings in check. When I start to feel you I will push you away and not let myself see you until those feelings begin to subside. You see I'm conscious of what I am doing and where I'm going at all the time."

"So, my feelings don't matter?"

"I'm sure they matter to you. You are the one that must protect your own heart and it is up to me and only me to avoid a possible heartbreak. No one can break my heart but me and I refuse to let that happen again in this lifetime."

"My efforts would be in vain?"

"I don't know. Talk is cheap. You may want to invest some time in pursuing me though. You never know what may happen," she said. "I may end up falling in love with a younger man."

"Do you have a problem with that?"

"Oh, shit. Fuck," she screamed. "No. Not when you're hitting it like that daddy. Oh my sweet Lord. You're going to make a liar out of me yet. What is it you want baby?"

We made good love and two of the three appointments that morning. Two of the places were buildings right on Edgecombe in Sugar Hill that Tuesday thought would be wonderful investments.

What I wanted was the loft across from hers or something similar to hers in close proximity. I didn't tell her that but that's what I wanted. She saw something different for me.

"If you take the loft across from me you'll be paying me rent. For a few dollars more you can let your tenants pay your rent as well as for the building and take in a small profit. It just makes good business sense to me."

I listened but when we returned and she showed me the loft I was sold. I understood what she was telling me but I simply fell in love with the potential the loft had. The only thing that bothered me was the close proximity to Tuesday. Still, she'd been explicit about separating business from pleasure so I didn't see her having any problem with our living arrangements.

"If the rent's reasonable I can still purchase the real estate. I'd just have to wait a little longer. I promise I'll have one of those buildings within a years time."

"I think we can do that."

"With your help I know we can do this," I said looking her straight in the eyes. I truly believed this.

Two weeks later I moved in and taking care of business. No longer did I take anything but my two hundred dollar clients and Tuesday in preserving me for herself suggested that I take on no more than three clients a week. I did as she suggested unless I had a special I couldn't turn down. A special was a client with special needs and wants and was willing to pay whatever amount to be satisfied in her own unique way. One woman gave me somewhere in the neighborhood of eight or nine hundred dollars for me to fondle and suck on her breasts. Some womens sho' had some strange cravings. When

I told Tuesday she simply played it off saying 'it is what it is' and customer service should be my only concern. It wasn't important what their particular fetish was but if it fit within my parameters just do it, deposit the money and keep it moving.

We talked and when we finished I came to the conclusion that women as a whole were stronger and more logical. I know that women are always thought to be more emotional and therefore more susceptible to acting on their feelings but I have to disagree. A woman may seem to be more emotional but once they come to a place where they have a plan and a direction women will remain steadfast in eliminating all else that is negative in their lives and kep only that which will allow them to progress. The women that I have come to know since I've been here are for the most part well-to-do with their heads screwed on right and seem pressed to lead me to the promised land. But they were so cold and calculating. Most of them had no problem calling and suggesting that we get together but other than that their lives remained a mystery. I had no real

affinity towards any of of my clients other than Tuesday but Tuesday even criticized that saying that if I left the door even slightly cracked I was opening it for potential problems. I heard her but I was too strong to be distracted or so I thought.

It was Tuesday who told me that and yet in the first two weeks I saw Tuesday whenever she had a spare moment. She brought in decorators, people to do the wall papering. She did all the interior decorating while I sat back and watched. She looked to

be taking a great deal of joy in doing so and by the time she was finished the loft looked amazing.

I began taking on clients as soon as she put the final touches on. I'd kept most of my client's numbers and most seemed glad to hear from me. I gave them my phone number and asked them to pass the word that I was back in business. Not a day later I had more calls than I could handle. Tuesday and I had already decided on no more than three clients a week but when the phone rang I saw dollar signs and soon had booked myself for the next twenty-eight days straight.

Tuesday was upset when I told her I'd booked myself for the entire month.

"You did what? I thought we agreed to go so slow the first

month. I was hoping you'd leave enough days open that we could test the waters with some newer, more up scale personnel and besides that you have to let your body rest up. It's extremely important that you take care of your body. Still, I don't know why you did it. You're not hurting for money."

I dropped my head. I'd let greed get in the way of my common sense.

"It was also very thoughtful of you. When you were booking your clients did you think about booking the woman across the hall from you? No. You didn't even consider that did you?"

"Today's Wednesday baby. My first client isn't until next Monday. That should leave us the rest of the week but if you need more time than that just let me know and I can call them back and reschedule."

"No. I guess I was just being selfish. And you're absolutely right. Don't let me get in the way of you and your livelihood."

"You would never have to let anything get between us if you'd commit to doing the right thing."

"And what is that?"

"Marry me."

"I thought we'd been down this road before."

"We have. You were supposed to mull it over and get back to me."

"I think that'sthat so flattering Marcus but come on man. I'm more than twice your age and on the downside of a good life. You need a nice young lady who can run with you and give you a house full of babies. Marriage, not that I take your proposal seriously, is a pretty serious matter Marcus and not one you should go handing out like invitations to a birthday party. There are a lot of us who really take the notion of marriage seriously so please don't throw it out there like it's just something to do when all else has failed."

The days were flying by and I still hadn't taken the time to call Kathryn. I was supposed to spend the second part of the week with her and I knew she was probably wondering why she hadn't heard from me.

I checked with Tuesday.

"Will you be wanting or needing me for anything else today sweetheart? I have some errands to run and some business I need to take care of."

"Would I be wanting you or needing you? Are you not listening to anything I'm saying? Hell, Marcus I'm still trying to decide how a fifty year old woman became involved with a twenty one year old and you want to know if I need or want you for the rest of the week. Of course I do. I want to feel your warmth laying next to me at night. There's nothing better than you and I holding each other for dear life in the wee hours of the morning. And then to awaken to see your beautiful facing staring, adoringly at me. How could I not want that? But don't mind me I'm just acting like a petulant teenager. You go ahead and handle your business before I regress further to being a toddler with a temper tantrum. By the way were you ever able to get in touch with Melissa?"

"I did. She met me at the docks on my arrival. And we spoke. I just wasn't all that specific."

"So, you didn't spell it out to her or even try to sell her on the idea? That crazy girl may be the key to your success. Did you tell her anything?"

"She picked me up at the docks when my ship pulled in. We wen't to her place and I left as soon as she passed out and came here."

It was the first time I'd seen Tuesday angry other than when I was teasing her in the bedroom but she was angry now.

"You know Marcus I keep asking myself why I even bother with you. You don't know and want to act like a responsible adult and each time you make a move we have to backtrack and do the whole damn thing all over again. And when I ask you to do something on your own behalf you just ignore me which is alright if you have a better plan for your future. I specifically asked you to sit down with Melissa. Melissa has access to a different clientele. She can introduce you to white clientele with deep pockets But instead you'd rather work for two hundred a night. I don't know why you're so insistent on trying to jump into something you know nothing about. Please tell me why it is so difficult for you to just let me take care of it. Trust me Marcus I will not let anything but good come to you if you would just trust me."

I didn't say a word. I couldn't. She was right. I was the student. I knew nothing and she was my teacher. I walked across the hall and brought back my planner.

"Call and reschedule all that need to be. Make sure that you're my first priority and pencil you in whenever you want to see me Tuesday. Call and tell Melissa your plan. I should be back no later than Saturday. If anything should come up call me. And, oh yeah, one more thing... I want you to know that I love you even if you can't find it in your cold, frozen heart to say 'I love you too,' I said closing the door and grabbing my overnight bag and heading out into the chilly, evening wind blowing in off the Hudson.

Knocking on the huge mahogany door on Edgecombe Avenue brought back memories although seeing Kathryn didn't bring back any good ones. Still, I needed to see her to bring about some closure. I didn't know if I was still in love with this woman who

had lied, used and stolen from me. I was torn between punishing her and making her somehow pay and praying to the good Lord Almighty that I was somehow mistaken and she was remorseful and had somehow changed. I didn't place much faith in the latter but I had to know.

"My God Marcus," Kathryn screamed as she opened the door smothering me with hugs and kisses. "Come in. Come in. My God Marcus you have really changed. You're a man now. My goodness. You have really filled out."

I smiled. Aside from gaining a couple of pounds I had to admit that she too looked better than before but I tried to stay focused. Unless she showed me something different she was just another client paying a large sum of money for my company.

"Are we staying here?"

"No, sweetheart. I'm just waiting for my driver. Now tell me. How have you been? You really do look fabulous. You've put a few pounds on and it really looks good on you. Did I say that? You're so muscular, so chiseled. You weren't like that when you left. But you still haven't told me how you've been."

"I'm good," I said smiling glad she was excited to see me. "Just been taking in the city since I've been back. It really has changed. In some ways it made me sorry I ever left," I said keeping my eyes on her.

"I wish you hadn't left either," she said letting her head rest on my shoulder.

"And why is that Kathryn?"

"Ahh, come on silly. You know why?"

"Flatter me anyway. Tell me why you were sorry to see me leave."

"Well, you know there are several reason why I didn't want to see you go but you left anyway. I thought we had good chemistry on a personal level and then we had business interests and the sky was the limit. And by the way and since we're on the subject why did you stop writing?"

"Because and although you seem to think we had good chemistry you never responded to my proposal. I thought that was both rude and disrespectful."

"Come on man! What woman do you know that would respond to a marriage proposal she receives by mail? But if that is your intent then I encourage you to court me the right way," she said crossing her leg and letting the split in her skirt fall exposing a chocolate, mocha thigh. "So, how are you making ends meet? Have you thought about when you might want to go back to work. I know you probably need a little time for rest and relaxation after the war but as soon as you're ready you let me know sweetie."

"I'm already on the job," I shot back laughing.

"Oh, I hate you," she said grinning back. "Come on are you ready?"

I felt good. There was little doubt in my mind that she was genuinely glad to see me. It warmed me to know that I was missed and missed by someone I looked up to and admired. I watched her as she went rushing about trying to gather her belongings.

"Just let me change my clothes and grab my bag. God it feels good to have you back."

"Say how did your friend make out? You know the one tat kept his eyes glued on my backside. You two were inseparable."

"Oh, you're referring to Henry Lucious. I just received a letter from him. He's having a ball. He went to Italy and fell in love with it. And the Italian women can't get enough of him. He's in heaven."

"So, he stayed on?"

"Yes. I'm telling you he absolutely loves it. He actually thinks he's contributing to the war effort. That and the fact that Italy ain't caught up in the whole Jim Crow thing. Made him think that he can stand tall represent his country and still be a man."

"And he's already tall," she commented making us both laugh. "Well, I'm glad your friend came into some good fortune. I just hope before the night is over I do as well," she said squeezing my thigh. We talked and laughed and reminisced about better days when life was simple and innocent.

"You know you left a week after you and I went to church that Sunday and I still had women calling me six months later. You left quite an impression but my question to you is are you ready to get back into the saddle?"

"I'm about to get back into the saddle of one of the finest lil' fillies in Harlem if I could just get her to be quiet and relax."

"Seriously though Marcus I know you have a little saved up but there's nothing but money and opportunity out there waiting for us. But let's not take it for granted. My father used to tell me that the worst thing in life is missed opportunity. I just don't want you to miss these opportunities."

"You're right. I agree and I will let you know when I'm ready but for right now I just want to feel my way around and see what's what and what opportunities avail themselves to me before I just jump back in. A friend of mine from the Army has a few connections with the railroad and I suspect I'm going to see if I can't be a Pullman Porter on the New York to Boston run. You know I'm just a simple boy from Georgia and I appreciate all that you've invested in me but I don't need a lotta money to be happy and the risks are kinda high when you think about it. That's what I have to think about. The risks all seem to fall on me as well as the work load."

Kathryn sat there stunned. I guess she never ever suspected anything like this from her young protege. Now I knew what sitting rooms were for. It was for stunned women to sit there and regain their thoughts. I could see the wheels turning in her head but I never expected what came out next.

"Nigga is you high? I hear tell that a lot of us go over to the war and get to smokin' and shootin' shit up and come back all fucked up. Is that what's happened to you? I know you just didn't say you wanted to be carrying white folks bags for them for tips? But you did say you were considerin' being a Pullman Porter didn't you?"

"I did."

"And you also mentioned something about marriage. You want me to consider marrying a Pullman Porter? Me? Kathryn Chapman who has struggled long and hard to rise up out of the bowels of Negrodom to marry down to one of the lowest jobs to be had by Negro men. Please tell me you're not serious. Please tell me you see something so much better for yourself Marcus. I see stardom for you. Do you have any idea of what I have planned for us? After a year or two I have you running for the city council right here in Harlem. Don't you see the possibilities are limitless. Our people need good strong lawyers to fight on their behalf. I see you fulfilling that role and I see us becoming fabulously rich," she said handing me her coat and pocketbook.

"Be a doll and take these upstairs while I grab a bottle of bubbly from the fridge," Kathryn said handing me her belongings."

I wondered why she needed anything. She was already tipsy but I did so. On the way up the stairs I heard Kathryn mumbling to herself.

'Railroad porter my ass! Stupid nigga. What is it that you don't understand boy? You are a cash cow. You're the goose that lay the golden egg and Kathryn's going to see just how many eggs you can lay," I heard her say before laughing out loud. "I'm coming sweetheart," she then yelled.

I'd heard enough to know the woman was uncaring, unfeeling and had no regard for my welfare but two could play this game and right now she was the cash cow that I

needed so badly if I were to achieve some of the goals that would free me from her and one day make me independent from her and all the other women I was now so dependent on.

Moments later, a broad grin spread across her face Kathryn handed me a glass.

"Is it still Chivas and milk?"

I smiled taking the glass. She was still grinning.

"You're certainly full of surprises. Picture that Ms. Kathryn, the wife of a Pullman Porter," she laughed almost spilling her drink. "That would be like snubbing your nose in God's face. He has bigger plans for you and I. Can't you you see he has blessed you by delivering you to me. You and I are going to make enough in the next two years to elevate you from your present position to something as promising and lucrative as law or politics. So, let there be no more talk of my baby totin' other people's bags. What we want is other people totin' yours. Now come here soldier and show me how much the Army taught you about the care and treatment of innocent civilians," Kathryn said smiling. But before I could fill her glass for her she was fast asleep. The following day Kathryn was up and about. When I asked her if our lovemaking was any better since the war and after a two year wait. I didn't seriously believe that Kathryn had waited two year's but if that's what she wanted me to believe then so be it.

"I don't recall us making love Marcus. I was quite tipsy but I would have remembered that especially after this long a wait. I think I was so excited that I drank a little too much. But we will deal with that later. Right now I need you to get your pretty ass up and get dressed," she said as she moved from one thing to another in a rush to get

her outfit together. She always looked like she stepped out of a fashion magazine and today was no different. But what made her especially appealing was that she was so bubbly and alive. To tell you the truth I had never seen her quite so excited. If I didn't know better I may thought that she missed me or perhaps she was just missing the goose that lay the golden eggs. However it translated it was fine with me.

My style had changed since being in Italy and I must admit I had grown rather fond of Italian suits and loafers. Kathryn like seeing me in them and agreed to take me shopping. After several hours of shopping down around Delancey Street I found myself the owner of a new wardrobe with seven new suits and four new pair of Italian loafers. Kathryn saw no problem in purchasing them and called it a welcoming home gift. She was unbelievable and the only problem she presented was persuading to let go of my arm and stand clear of me so the tailor could measure me.

"Did I tell you that I was a little skeptical about your plan to raise prices but when I finally gathered the courage to tell them that there had been a raise in prices I didn't hear one complaint instead they wanted to know when they could get an appointment but since I hadn't spoken to you I couldn't book 'em. I did sorta overstep my liberties in one case.

But I met this lil' girl who came with her husband from down around your way. I believe it was Georgia. Well, anyway she and her husband came here and rented a flat from me. That same week Uncle Sam shipped her husband overseas. He didn't last a week. Anyway, she received her little condolences package. She doesn't want to go back to

Georgia and so as a part of her grief therapy counseling she joined our group. Now a few of the women in our group have used you in granting closure and she didn't seem to object and booked you for two nights despite the new prices. I was shocked but for that type of money I had to book her even if I had to strap up," Kathryn laughed. "But seriously if you want it let me know."

"What type of money are we talking?"

"Eight hundred."

"I hate to turn down that type of money but you asked me for this time. Lord knows I could use the money but like I said this is your time."

"Don't you worry about me baby. You go ahead and make this money for us. What kind of woman would I be to stand between a man and his money?"

"You sure Kathryn?"

"Yes. It's all fair in love and war. The girl outbid me. Besides I ain't never had that type of money to spend on no man for no sex. Once it gets to be that expensive I may just have to marry that there fellow. When I study the cost and convenience of having my own full time live in dick I can't even compete. And that's what it looks like it's coming to. So, it looks like marriage is the only option if I want to see and spend time with you. Am I right?"

I smiled.

"Well, Kathryn being that this is your brainchild I do believe I'm going to let you figure this one out on your own darlin'."

"You're not serious."

"I do believe that you were the one that taught me to never let emotions interfere with business."

"I did but I think in this case it's okay to make an exception. You have to remember that I haven't seen you in two years and..."

"And I'm your cash cow so call her and confirm her for tomorrow. Give her my number so we can set up a place to meet."

"Where are you staying these days Marcus?"

"I'm staying with some Army buddies out on the island temporarily."

"Why don't you move in here until you find just what it is you're looking for. You never know. You may find it right here."

"I will give that some serious thought," I smiled. "But since you have me working tomorrow let me get out of here so I can get some rest before I see what's her name."

"Jennifer. Jennifer Green."

"Tell me a little about her."

"What's to tell? I'd say she's in her late twenties, early thirties. She's quite attractive and I'd say she's been widowed a little over a year. She's a little country girl. She reminds me alot of you when we first met. Simple and innocent. Y'all should hit it off right nice. But like I said I really don't know alot about her. Coffee?"

"No, I'm good and thank you for everything Kathryn. I'll be in touch the first chance I get."

"You owe me Marcus. Don't let me have to come collecting."

I closed the large mahogany door behind me and thought about the times not too long ago where Henry Lucious and I would fantasize about Ms. Kathryn and here I'd just walked away from her with her wanting me. How life had changed. And I thought to myself. It could be worse.

With seven suits and two shopping bags full of shoes I made it down to 8th Avenue where I hailed a cab. Minutes later I was back at my place. As soon as I got off the elevator there was T.

"Thought you'd never get back baby." Noticing the garment bags I could see the anger and contempt in her eyes.

"I see someone took good care of my baby. Do they have a name?"

"Why play games. You know exactly who bought those suits. There's only one person who would buy me those suits."

"You know I would have bought you those suits if you'd only ask me to." T said. "You know I would have."

"You probably would have but I would have never asked you to. And I didn't ask for these. You know me better than that Tuesday."

A deliberate tear forced it's way down her cheek.

"Marcus."

"Yes Tuesday."

"Can I ask you a question?"

"Yes."

"Why did you feel a need to go and see her after all the wrong and awful things she's done to you?"

"I'm not sure. I guess I don't want it to be true. Perhaps I'm hoping and praying that I was mistaken. Maybe I'm hoping that the years have changed her or that she's having some remorse. I guess I was just looking for closure."

"And has she changed?"

"I hardly think so but as of tonight I will have closure one way or another."

"How's that? What are you up to Marcus?"

"She booked an upscale client for two nights for eight hundred of which I am to receive seven hundred and twenty dollars minus her so-called finders fee. I told her to have the client call me to set up a place to meet. But what I'm really interested in knowing is how much she really charged her. Then I can tell if she can or cannot be trusted."

"And if everything comes up smelling roses then what? You mean then you'll know if it's alright to still be in love with her?"

I didn't answer. Instead I took the glass from T and walked across the hall where I ran a hot bath and was satisfied to linger peacefully. The glass of wine warmed me and I was tempted to go and ask Tuesday if refills were free but I didn't need or want the drama. Besides they had the same wine down at the corner store and I could be back

within a few minutes and avoid the drama. I loved Tuesday and knew all she was interested in was my best interest but tonight I was exhausted. Yes that's what I'd do. Approaching the front door I could not ignore the note. It read.

'Spoke to Melissa after you left. She agreed to help us out for a small cost. There's always a small cost.

I apologize for my behavior earlier and if you're not too upset with me I'd like to make it up to you if you're free tonight. If not I understand and will keep that in account the next time I decide to act like a jealous lil school girl."

I wondered if this was going to be a problem. My question was quickly answered when T opened the door. Standing there looking as radiant as I had ever seen her. T stood there in a sheer whit negligee her taut brown body straining to get loose. I could feel myself growing erect. Noticing the bulge in my suit pants T opened the door wider.

"I really wanted to talk but from the looks of things that may have to wait. I see you have some other things on your mind. No problem," she said grabbing me by the hand and pulling me down the long hallway to her bedroom.

She received no argument from me. She did that to me. She may have not been the finest woman I knew. She may not have even been the finest fifty year old I knew but out of all the women I knew she had that special something that did it for me. There was no doubt that I was in love in a profession where love was often discounted. Yes, she did that to me. The last person I 'd felt like this for was Kathryn. They both had that affect on me. And the funny thing about it was that everyone knows that familiarity breeds contempt but it was just the opposite in Tuesday's case. The more time I spent with her the more desirable she became. She'd become my partner and best friend just like Henry Lucious with a whole lot more than H.L. could have ever offered.

Still, the tears were a bit extreme. She'd already told me that in my profession you never worked and played in the same place, never cross boundaries she'd warned me. And never but never mix business and emotions and yet isn't that what she'd done? I felt confused and betrayed.

She'd said what she had to say and taken the upper hand now that we were in the bedroom. Getting on top she rode me like there was no tomorrow and until she had me screaming her name. She was the only woman I knew that could leave me begging, craving. She did that to me. Making love to her had always been different even from the very beginning. I guess you might say we were equally yoked or so I thought until tonight when I knew that she had only allowed me to think that. I begged her to finish but she was teasing me, punishing me and then she stopped.

"You like the way T makes you feel don't you? And because you like the way T makes you feel I have some news for you Marcus. I will not be paying you for your services anymore. In fact, I'm not paying for anything anymore. And if you want to see me in the future you will ask me out on a date. Do you understand?"

I was too shocked to respond and after she'd orgasmed she got up and headed for the bathroom. I followed her into the bathroom and sat on the toilet while she showered.

"What's wrong baby?"

"If you must know I've broken all the rules."

"I'm lost. What are you talking about?"

"Come on man. Isn't it obvious Marcus?"

"Am I missing something?"

"Yes. Dammit. Can't you see that I've fallen in love with you?" she screamed. "I can only imagine how strange that must somehow sound coming from a woman old enough to be your mother Marcus. Marcus."

"I'm here sweetheart. I'm just waiting for you o get out of the shower."

"You're not going to hit me. Are you Marcus? I apologize for disrespecting you."

"Disrespecting me? You've got to be kidding me." I said as I took her in my arms and hugged her as tightly as I could. "I am honored that you should think so highly of me. I've felt the same way since I got home. I would have said something but I didn't want to jeopardize our friendship. So, to me it was better or at least seemed better to have you as my friend than to lose you altogether."

"Oh, Marcus, tell me that's not the way you really saw it?"

"I did. But now since I know baby let me ask you a question I've been wanting to ask you for a long time."

"By all means, please do," Tuesday muttered wiping the tears from her face.

I paused. I was delighted to hear that this older woman who had seen the world and been exposed to so much more than I had actually fallen for a country boy like me but was this what I wanted to do? For all of her attributes I still wasn't sure. I'd fantasized about this very day for I don't know how long but I still had apprehensions. I wanted children and Tuesday was far past her childbearing years and I'd always dreamed of having kids.

"Having second thoughts?"

"Second thoughts? No. I'm way beyond that."

"It ain't easy is it?"

"No. But I've found that the best things in life are never easy. But they can be easier with you by my side."

"Oh my. Marcus what are you saying?"

"I think that's pretty obvious T. I want to spend the rest of my life with you. I want to marry you. I want you to be my wife Tuesday?"

There was a time when no words were spoken between us. To say there was an uncomfortable silence would be an understatement. I wondered if she was simply playing with me. If there was one thing I'd gotten to know listening to them was that all women were devious. Was this just her way of making me open up and confess my feelings towards her? After all, what would a wealthy socialite want or need with the likes of me? I found out that evening as Tuesday took me to places and drove me to places I'd never in my life been.

I considered that night our honeymoon even though Tuesday still hadn't replied to my proposal of marriage. Nothing had changed since our initial encounter. I knew that I was in love. She was a client. But there was a difference between T and the rest of my clients. It was umistakeable. And I felt it each and every time. Now it was out in the open and although she'd forced the conversation she had no response when he admitted his love for her. Now who was having second thoughts?

"Tuesday. Are you awake."

"Yes, dear."

"You admit that you love me but you're still not sure that you want to marry me. Is that what I'm to believe?"

"Oh Marcus I do love you and I'm still very much a woman no matter how hard I come off but now that you ask me I'm not sure that I can handle all these women leaving my man's house after giving themselves to him. Look at me. I went in with the idea of scratching an itch and came out in love. I don't think that's unusual and now I'm just supposed to sit idly by while your'e making love to another lonely, lovesick woman waiting for her knight in shining armor to come by and sweep her off her feet just like you did to me."

"Well, I don't know if this will put your mind at ease or not but aside from you I don't particularly enjoy it and as soon as I receive my real estate license I'll be fine. You know I start classes on Monday."

"Yes I do. But you need to work at least two years before you can invest enough so that it will sustain you and in the meantime I guess I'm supposed to standby and watch some rather well-healed, lonely women make you offers and place bids for your time the same way I did. And as you know for every person there is always someone who can do it better out there. I don't know if I can just standby and wait to be replaced."

"Hasn't happened yet."

"Hasn't it? I do believe that's why Kathryn's sitting home bristling now and

you're here with me."

"Only time will tell but all I ask is that you command me my princess and I will do as you ask. All I'm asking is for the opportunity to be a part of your life."

"And I will try to my love but I want you to know that I have no control when it comes to someone disturbing my inner sanctum and once I claim you I won't have any control or problem in eradicating one of these bitches who crosses the line. Just thought you should know."

"We will find one way or another to manipulate this quagmire we've created."

"With God's help."

"Yes. With His help we will not only survive but prosper."

"In spite of..."

"It could be worse."

"Yes. It can always be worse."

We spent that night together and decided that my place would only be used for work. I knew she was uncomfortable with the whole arrangement but I tried to go about it as professionally as possible. Hell, all I could do was try and pray.

Jennifer called later that evening.

"Hello Marcus. This is Jennifer. Jennifer Green. Ms. Kathry asked that I call you."

"Hi Jennifer."

"Hi Marcus. Ms. Kathryn told me to call for the time and address."

I gave her the information before asking her point blank.

"I just need to confirm everything to make sure we're all on the same page. What did Kathryn charge you for the two nights?"

"Oh. She charged me eleven hundred for the two nights. A thousand for our time together and another hundred for the facilities."

"And how did you pay her?"

"I met her at Macy's this morning and paid her in cash. Is everything okay?"

"No, but it will be. I'll talk to you more when I see you."

"Looking forward to it."

"I am as well," I said before hanging up.

Kathryn had done it again. Our first business venture in two years but she hadn't changed. She'd collected eleven hundred dollars from Jennifer and I'd gotten a paltry seven hundred and twenty dollars. And it wasn't the four hundred that she'd skimmed off the top. It was the fact that she didn't value our relationship enough to be honest. I couldn't trust her to be honest and up front and no business arrangement could ever exist without trust. It hurt because I had entrusted her with my everything with blind faith that she would teach me and take me to the next level. Well, she'd taught me alright. She taught me that everything isn't always what it seems.

I learned that just because you love someone there was no guarantee that they would reciprocate and return your love. I learned that often times when you expressed your love it only showed a vulnerability an invitation for certain people to take that

vulnerability or weakness and use it to take advantage and exploit you. That was Kathryn. I loved her and this is how she repayed me. I had hoped she changed but there was no change. There were only higher stakes and she had her sights on me to take her there. I, on the other hand, wanted desperately to see some change, some remorse, some love, something but I saw nothing but the same ol' and more of the same.

When I told Tuesday she did her best to take the high road.

"So, I guess with this latest transgression you now have the closure you so desperately needed."

"I wish I could say that but I'm angry. How does she think she can just take advantage of people like that? She needs to be made to pay!"

"I understand how you feel but sometimes you just have to chalk things up. Call it a learning experience and let it go. Remember Him who said 'Let vengeance be mine'."

"Well, from what I'm told He's a little busy and would welcome the help."

"Listen Marcus. I'm going to need you to listen and pay close attention to what   I'm going to tell you."

She was serious now.

"You must learn to pick and choose your battles. Every battle should not be fought. Every battle is not winnable. You must choose the battles that will enable you to win the war. This is not one. I've known Kathryn for a lot of years. There is no good in

her and she is dangerous. That's all I can tell you. She can make your life very difficult if you oppose her. You take it from there but please don't let me get caught up in anything between you and Kathryn. I do my best to steer clear of her. I know who she is and what's she's about. You're just finding out."

"I hear you," I said angrily but I really wasn't listening. She'd stolen from me again and I was hot.

"Listen. Call it even. What did she spend on your clothes. Over a grand I'm sure so you're even. And I want you to start wearing those suits she bought and we'll pick up a couple more at the end of the week. Image is everything. After your class tomorrow I want you to ride out on the island with me. I have a group of rather well-to-do white women who would like to purchase an old abandoned warehouse that my daddy left me. I want to sell both you and the warehouse at the same time. I don't need you to be anything but who you are now save the angry scowl. Women love the strong silent type.

I'm going to introduce you as my 'assistant', smile, and then say that this is not your typical assistant. He does quite a bit more than assist me with my paperwork. If you'd like to more about his other attributes just take a card. But let me tell you ladies. We had an auction where we auctioned off Marcus for the night for the Knights of Columbus in Bay Shore and this young man went for five grand. So, if your light bill is due you may not want to call. He's not cheap."

They all laughed and I was shocked at how many gave me the once over before picking up a card. We were working in unison and I was really glad to know she was in my corner.

Kathryn. Well, she was another story but Tuesday was right. She was dangerous. If there was to be any type of retribution on my part it had to be swift and debilitating with no hint of where it came from. But before any of that I was sure we could and should address the problem, gain some acknowledgment and be civil in ending our business arrangement. If nothing else I wanted her to know that the jig was up. She'd been caught red handed. And so despite T's advice I called.

"Kathryn."

"Hey sweetie. How are you? I was wondering when I'd be hearing from you. I was just thinking how I let you get away from me and left me standing empty handed. My girlfriends been throbbing since you left. And yes I'm home and I'm soaking wet and will probably only get worse being on the phone with you. Come on sweetie you can squeeze me in for a quickie. I'll leave the front door open. How long will it take you baby?"

"I wish I was calling under better circumstances."

"Why hon? What's wrong?"

"I just spoke to Jennifer Green."

"And?"

"And she tells me that you charged her a thousand dollars for me and another hundred for the facilities."

"Why that little lyin' bitch. Marcus you know she's lying. How long have we known each other? Almost three years and have I ever taken a dime from you?"

"Well, now that you bring it up the only other person I talked to was Tuesday and she told me the same thing."

"Don't listen to them. Them bitches are lying. Tuesday has always been jealous of me," she screamed.

"Kathryn listen to me. Neither of them know each other or about our conversations yet there is one common denominator and that is you. Both told the same story. Why is that? Is it some kind of conspiracy where everyone is after Kathryn? The fact is you've not been honest with me. I trusted you and you stole from me so the only thing I can suggest in order to protect myself is that we terminate all business ties. I will not service Jennifer under such conditions and I suggested she go back to you for a refund. You lied to her and to me. Goodbye Kathryn. I wish you much luck and success."

I then pretended to hang up as she continued to rant and rave about how she molded me into the person I am today and this was the thanks she got. I was an awkward little country boy who she groomed to be a New York gentleman. And then I heard her say something I didn't know she owned.

"I taught you everything you know nigga. Two days ago I put over a thousand dollars worth of clothes on your back. What you don't seem to get is that's up to me whether you work or not. If I find you trying to procure dates behind my back or even catch you with another woman I will kill you. I don't care if it's your mother. I will kill you."

"Goodnight Kathryn."

"Just remember. You belong to me Marcus. Fuck with me and I will kill you."

I recounted the phone call to T.

"She's quite capable you know."

"I would have never thought that was a part of who she was."

"And believe me that is a part of her. That's who she is. That's why I told you to leave it alone. Not only have you challenged her authority but now you are a threat to that good sister's name throughout the community. She has to either shut you up or get rid of you. She'll be playing hardball from here on out."

"Seriously?"

"Seriously but I don't want you to worry about her. I'll take care of your security for now and until we can work out a truce or a buyout."

"A buy out? What are you saying T?

"Yeah, a buy out. We'll give her a few grand and ask her to release you and go from there."

"I will not. I don't owe her."

"You will pay her. What will it take for you to get it through your thick head that Kathryn is not someone to be toyed with. Do as she says and move on with your life, our lives."

"It's the principle of the whole thing Tuesday. She's been stealing from me the entire time and now you want me to pay her more so she can't steal anymore."

"Marcus."

"Yes."

"Do you love me?"

"I do."

"Then do this for me."

The following day I rode out to Montauk Point with Tuesday after class. She'd been tutoring me so class

seemed redundant. But the real joy to me was watching Tuesday manipulate these rich white women

into purchasing the dilapidated warehouse before us.

"Ladies, do not look at what you see as an old warehouse but the future home and headquarters of The

Women of Montauk Point." she said and they all cheered wildly. Wine was poured. And Tuesday

looking better than any woman there in her navy blue, business suit and matching heels had Thomas the

driver pull out a wooden facsimile of the remodeled warehouse which read W.M.P in bronze letters

across the top.

On the way back home Tuesday turned and smiled at me before digging into her purse and handing me a folded piece of paper. Opening it I realized it was a check and not only was it a check it was a check for two hundred and fifty thousand dollars. What it was was more money than I could even imagine. But it wasn't the money that really intrigued me. It was the selling. It was having every angle covered by knowing your merchandise and being knowledgeable. You could sell if you left no stone unturned and

knew all that there was to know about your product and Tuesday was knowledgeable. And these were the results. We left there with a two hundred and fifty thousand commission off of one piece of property and I was hooked. Arriving at home some hours later I gathered the few purchases I'd picked up during the day. Thomas was grabbing the rest of the packages from the trunk and Tuesday was already at the the door to the house when shots rang out. I couldn't move. And then I thought about T and dropped and ran to my baby. Shots were still being fired but it didn't matter. T was down on one knee but she hadn't been hit. Dresses and scarves adorned the sidewalk.

"Check on Thomas, Marcus," she said trying to compose herself but Thomas was unscathed. The only shots fired that had been in Tuesday's direction.

A car screeched as it pulled off but I couldn't make out the faces of the passengers. And just like that it was over.

"You okay T?"

"I'm fine Marcus. Why don't you give Thomas a hand. I'm sure he's shook."

I did as I was told and met Thomas across the street at the limo. He hardly seemed shook as he leaned against the car smoking a cigarette.

"Don't be surprised Marcus. This is not the first time Ms. Frazier has been under fire from this person if I think I'm correct about who's behind this."

"And who do you think was behind this Thomas?"

"This is between you and me Marcus. I ain't tryna get you involved.

Do you understand? Now tell me. Who was behind this?"

"Can't be no other than Ms. Kathryn. She and Ms. Tuesday used to be terribly close but not long after you left for the war things soured between them something awful. This is not the first time she's sent Ms. Tuesday a warning."

"And you're not worried?"

"No. I seen people when they want to get rid of someone. But that don't seem the intent when it comes to Ms. Kathryn getting rid of Ms. Tuesday. I think Ms. Kathryn's just tryna send a message and only them two know what's really going on. I heared some time ago where these three young cats tried to rob Ms. Kathryn's during some church function. Kathryn told the churchgoers to give the robbers all their valuables to make sure no one was hurt. The police had no leads and it looked like that was the end of it. A few weeks later the New York Post ran an article about three Negro boys being beaten in their apartment gangland style. There was a note attached to each. It read. 'No man shall steal from God's house.' We all knew who beat them boys. But no I ain't worried. Ms. Tuesday can take care of herself. Did you see those rich white women open their checkbooks today? She plays high stakes poker everyday. Trust me she can handle this. This is nothing new to her."

"Thanks Thomas." I said shaking his hand before following Tuesday into the apartment building.

Tuesday busied herself trying on her newly purchased garments.

"You okay T?"

"Never been better," she said grinning and holding up her commission check. "You see Marcus. Become adept with your craft and earn. Ignore all the rest of the distractions and keep it moving. That's what I keep trying to get you to understand."

"Baby, do you realize that someone just shot at you?"

"Yes and?"

"Do you know why someone would try to shoot you?"

"Yes, and you do too. I tried to tell you she was dangerous but you wouldn't listen."

"Oh my God. I'm so sorry T. Would you like me to speak to her?"

She turned and I knew she wasn't happy with me.

"I you think you've said enough already Marcus."

I've never felt so bad but T was right. I should have never said anything. I should have left the whole affair just pass over. But this was too much.

"So, you really think Kathryn was behind all of this?"

"Come on man."

"Seriously?"

"I tried to tell you she was dangerous Marcus."

"But shooting at us?"

"She's just letting you and I know not to mess with the order of things."

"And?"

"I don't want you to worry about things Marcus. I'll take care of Kathryn. All I want you to do is worry about your schooling and business. Can you do that for me?"

I nodded. Hadn't I caused enough problems already?

"Let's try it my way this time and see how we fare?"

I said nothing. From what Thomas told me this went further than what was transpiring now and so I thought it perhaps wise to let Tuesday handle the present situation. Besides when I tried to resolve it civilly this had been the results.

"Sweetheart. Don't you have a client tonight?"

"Yes. I have one at eight."

"Okay. Well, come find me before you go to class in the morning."

"Can't wait."

"I have a little business tonight. Gonna see if I can firm up the security around here and gonna put a few feelers out to see what the word is on the street. Then I'm going to a reception downtown. I shouldn't be home too late."

"And you're telling me this why?"

"In case you sneak out in the middle of the night 'cause you get to missing me so much. Just wanted you to rest easy if you don't find me where you think I'm supposed to be."

"Let me not find you there," I said grabbing her and kissing her passionately. "Damn I just found you and already you're telling me that you're not going to be there for me?"

"Just informing you Marcus. With this crazy woman on the rampage I think it's important we stay in touch as much as possible."

"I hear you. But you know T, between school, work and the gym you should know my schedule by heart."

"There you go again. Just make sure I have access to you at all times Marcus."

The night tended to be the same as most nights. I hate to generalize but whatever afflicted most of the women that came to be clients was their phobia for sex. I don't know where it had it's inception but the affliction ran deep and was widespread. Most of my clients were beautiful women and I'm talking in spirit each uniquely different and not one of them lacking for anything but a good man. I'd even venture to say that if they had been valued and treated fairly I would not be employed but for a cost I served a purpose and allowed them to be catered too the way they should have been catered to. Still, they were all missing the quintessential ingredient. They were missing love. In fact, I didn't know of one woman that wasn't aside from Tuesday.

It was easy for me to separate the two. I loved Tuesday. In fact I loved her so much that it frightened me at times. I'd loved before and wound up sadder than I'd ever been in my life. It's been years and I still can't bear to think about it. I never want to go

through that again and yet the deeper I fall in love with this woman only, the greater the possibility of my world coming to a thunderous end. I don't know if I could endure another cataclysmic upheaval in my life at this point. And yet Tuesday draws me closer everyday. There is no mention of my work. I go across the hall, return in the morning to get ready for class and return to either stay at home or cross the hall that evening. It's if nothing else different but it's funny to me how something may appear one way until you step into the shoes of the man running that race. Each day I go to work and pray no one passes judgment on what it is that I do. At first I enjoyed it. It was different. I was a teenager who yesterday couldn't, for whatever reason, procure sex no matter how hard I persevered. The next day women of note were paying to have sex with me. For a nineteen year old colored boy that ain't never had nothing that was something. But the years had begun to accumulate and now all the faces became one wonderfully, beautiful bronze weathered old woman's face that cried from grief from too long suffering at the hands of he who was put here to love her and to be the mother of his children. She had little in the way of faults or defects yet she had been cast all the hurt and humiliations that came with her fate. I took her money and tried to replace some small segment of what was missing in their lives. I admired them. I admired their strength and how they continued on despite everything and from their strength I too gained strength.

I watched Tuesday and I knew that she too wanted the fairy tale with the fairy tale ending every little girl dreams of. And because she'd grown older didn't mean the dream

had somehow been deferred. No. It may have been tucked away in storage but there was no reason to believe that it had been deferred. But the fact that there were women in her building virtually every night with her man was something that I did not know if I could necessarily fathom if the shoe were on the other other foot. Was this some sort of strength and fortitude to look pass the immediate transgression in order to see the end of the road. Was this the same strength the slave had after the master had relinquished her to nothing? Whatever it was Tuesday said nothing although I felt her torment. And the more I felt the more I tried to love her and show her that she was the only queen I needed.

I remembered her taking her to dinner and then taking her to see the American Negro Theater's first production, 'On Striver's Row'.

Many of Tuesday's friends were there and there were quite a few people I hadn't seen since before the war and I soon realized that this may have not been the best idea.

Not long after our appearance I received a phone call.

"I so hoped I would hear from you and we could put the past behind us Marcus. But the only thing I'm hearing is that you are working with a whole new set of high end clientele and attending opening nights where tickets couldn't even be had by me. Now my question is if young Marcus is going to openly defy me after I told me that he either worked for me or he would not work. I was informed that you were escorting Tuesday Frazier to the opening after I specifically told you that you would not see any former clients. Did I not specifically tell you that you were finished and they were off limits?"

I was upset by this point and wanted to ask her who the hell she thought she was and tell her where she could go but I'd promised Tuesday and so I apologized.

"I heard you and I understand you Kathryn but you know I hadn't been doing anything except working for the last few months. Yeah, I got the job as a Pullman Porter and that's all I do is work so when I got a weekend off I called one of the only people I know from the old days and asked her if she'd accompany me to the play. There wasn't anything to it other than that."

"Better not have been. Now why haven't I seen you. You still owe me a date. The last time I saw you you were running off with that little bitch that said I short changed you. Why don't you come and see me Mr. Pullman Porter?"

"I've been planning on it. I pull out tomorrow for Boston and then off to Chicago. I should be back the middle of next week. I'll give you a call then."

"I look forward to hearing from you Marcus."

I didn't have to work thanks to Tuesday reworking my schedule and she had a Japanese cook come in and prepare dinner. Over dinner we talked.

"What's going on with the whole Kathryn thing T?"

"Not much. She's kind of low key right now. Not much going on on her end. And that's a good thing. Why do you ask?"

"She called me."

"And?"

"I lied to her. Told her I'd been working so much so when I had a day off I just wanted to get out and my coworker gave me two tickets so I called you."

"And she went for that?"

"You asked me not to antagonize her."

"You did well Marcus but I have to agree with you. This is crazy. Do you realize that's the first time in four months that we have been out together? I do believe it's time we had a little sit down with Sister Kathryn. I also think it's time we started putting a portfolio together for you. You have a little over sixty thousand in the bank. I think we can start looking at a few pieces of prime real estate."

I smiled.

"Kathryn. Tuesday here."

"Hey girl. I figured I'd be hearing from you. What is it I can do for you? You getting an itch you need scratched?"

"Not exactly. Wow! I guess it has been awhile. No. I'm afraid those days are over. I have someone permanently that's quite capable of scratching any itch I may have."

"Is that right? Girl you know kidnaping is illegal so untie whoever you have taken hostage."

I had to laugh.

"Seriously, Kathryn. I've gotten engaged since I last saw you."

"Well, damn girl if anyone deserves it you do. You've crossed the half a century mark haven't you? Shit. Lord knows you've put your time in. So, who is he? Do I know the lucky fellow?"

"No. But listen that's not why I called you."

"What's up?"

"Marcus called me and asked me to meet with him yesterday to discuss your hold on him. He wants you to release him. The kid went from a gigolo to a Pullman Porter. He doesn't want to be pimped Kathryn. All he wants is to go to work everyday. Get married. Have a couple of babies and buy a house in Queens."

"And all that's fine when I'm finished with him. But right now the boy's got some work to put in. He owes me. I'm saying he took things from me and didn't complete his assignment and that was with no other than me."

"He explained and I understand Kathryn. I don't want to revisit the negatives. All he asked me to do was to speak with you and see what it would take for you to release him."

"I have to laugh. We can't even begin to talk until he fulfills his previous obligation. Let's just see right through here if he has any remorse and if he's ready to correct his mistakes. Let him ask for forgiveness and the we'll see about releasing him. He has three days Tuesday. He knows my number."

"So, that's it. I have to kow tow to her wants and desires as well as be apologetic for two days and then she just might consider releasing me. And all the time I though that freedom came with emancipation."

"Different rules. Different game."

"I suppose but what gets me is tact that she really believes that she can demand that I sex her and because she can force me she somehow believes that I will like it and succumb to it and she can and will control me with it."

"You know Marcus I love you more than life itself and it's no easy thing for me to be at home in my bed at night to know that the man I love is across the hall doing to some other woman what I wish he was doing to me. Oh my God! You can't imagine and I know a man such as yourself could not do it. But I endure. I compartmentalize shit is what I do and I watch Marcus shower me with anything he thinks I might like just to constantly remind me that across the hall doesn't matter. And do you know why?

Because Marcus repeats this everyday for this chocolate brown fifty three year old he says he loves. And for that reason I can endure. But this bitch is really pushing me. She wants me to send my man to her so she can have her way with him and then promise him the world if he can once again gather the reins. Well, what choice do we have?"

I did not answer. She was not asking me and suddenly I saw the light click.

"Call her and schedule her for tomorrow. Take care of her and offer her nothing and accept nothing from her. That part will be done. And all that will be left should be your buyout and we will be done once an all with her."

Her face was radiant.

"Have you seen Thomas today?"

"Yes. I saw him about a half an hour ago in the library."

"He absolutely loves the library. I really do think he uses it more than anyone else. Do me a favor and see if you can't round him up and send him to me."

As predicted Thomas sat in the library, leg crossed, pipe in mouth and book in hand. Seeing me approach he stood and grinned.

"This is the quietest place in the house with the most going on," he chuck

led.

"Sorry to interrupt you Thomas but Ms. Tuesday would like to see you."

The older man scurried off in the direction of the kitchen. I sat down at the huge mahogany desk that sat in the middle of the library and dialed Kathryn. We agreed to meet that night. She seemed anxious and I just wanted to get it over with and move passed her.

And after Tuesday gave me all the do's and don'ts for the third time I left. Arriving at her home minutes later I was shaken to find her in mink coat and heels. As

soon as I closed the door she let the coat fall exposing her naked body to me. I stood there in awe. And she took it from there. She reminded me of Tuesday in that matter taking me to new heights and I could only wonder where all this passion had been. Had she let it lay dormant for times such as these or had it just been that long? I didn't know. We made love for much of the night and when she came for the last time she turned to me and laughed.

"I will never release you Marcus. You will always be mine."

She rolled over and went to sleep after that and I thought of some of my buddies overseas. I remember them really being dogged by one particularly racist officer. By the next morning a sad misfortune had befallen him. I thought of snapping her neck and making it look like a robbery but I didn't have it in me and T had given me explicit instructions on how to handle Kathryn.

"I really want you to see if you can't make her fall in love with you Marcus."

"And how will that help us come to a buyout?"

"Well, I sincerely doubt that she's going to let us buy her out but I do believe you that if you use that same charm that you used on me that there's a good chance she may give you everything."

"That's a leap."

"It may be. But give her the impression that you are still head over heels with her and are and have been torn up by her decision not to marry you. Let her know that her

rejection has left you a battered and broken man. And let's see how we appear after that. Beg her to allow you to come see her Thursdays. Tell her it's your only day back in the city."

"Damn baby. You broke the bone in my back last night. That was well worth the wait Marcus but now let me ask you something."

"Anything."

"Well, you owe me another night but I don't think I want to take advantage of that tonight. I think that I've had enough of you to last me for quite some time but I want to be honest with you. I played the love game for quite awhile, you know looking for Mr. Right and always came up empty. I guess it just wasn't meant for me. I don't know. Maybe I'm just too high maintenance for too many of the colored boys. I'm thinking the state senate and they're considering being porters. But I do know one of the things I like about having a man is the sex and you my dear certainly bring that. And you're mine. What the hell thinks that you can buy yourself out? And why would you when I'm paying you and bringing this fine brown frame to give you some of the best love in New York City." she smiled.

Two hours later Tuesday was on the phone with her.

"Ten thousand and you release him."

"He must mean an awful lot to you to pay ten grand for him. How does your fiancee feel about you paying for some other man's release? Or does he even know?"

I had to ignore her remarks. It was Kathryn's way to take evil nasty swipes in an effort to anger and once angry and all control gone she'd pick you apart. No. It was important to stay focused and cool and on topic.

"Damn you Kathryn! Ten grand is a fair price."

"And who's trying to be fair. I'm trying to profit from something someone wants and that's Marcus. I thought we'd agree to hold all discussion until after we've consummated our other dealings. I don't know if he told you or not but he wore this ol' girl out. I know I had to come at least eleven or twelve times. I couldn't possibly do that on back-to-back nights. Did he make you come like that when he first got back? Oh my God. He's not like before either. He's really hung now. But anyway I'll give you a call after our next play date."

She was playing with us now, stringing us along but it was Tuesday who cautioned patience and reserve. I felt like a caged animal forced to stay inside for anything other than school and the gym. It was a very rigid and disciplined existence and

probably the best thing for me at this juncture in my life. Tuesday controlled everything and I was learning at breakneck speed so I really didn't mind the restraints placed upon me.

And though I had no idea of what was really going on between the two women I had the utmost faith in Tuesday exacting the victory in the end.

"Force her into another quick date. Tell her it's on you, that you just want to be with her, see her... You know what I'm talking about. Charm her ass Marcus."

I grabbed T's tiny frame off the floor and took her in my arms. I didn't want to hear another word about Kathryn. I did however call her after T and I had made love.

"I'm just now starting to get back to normal but if you say you need me to see me then I'm here for you."

"Thursdays."

"What about Thursday? Tomorrow's Thursday and I agreed. You just haven't given me a time."

"No Kathryn. Every Thursday. I want to spend my every Thursday, my everyday off back here in the city with you."

"Goodness. And just think that a couple of days ago you were talking of a buy out."

"That was two years without us making love."

"Oh, Marcus was I that good?"

"You weren't the same person I left before the war."

"Is that good?"

"Is it? After being with you Sunday I knew I had to try again. I need to have you but not like we were before. I know you don't care for my occupation and see so much more for me but I hope you respect what makes me happy. I enjoy traveling and seeing

new and different things. I'm not like you Kathryn. I'm happy with the simple things. A good book. The baseball game. It doesn't take much. I'm a porter that has a couple of dollars saved and I've been in love with you since I first met you. All I'm hoping for is that you allow yourself the possibility to fall in love with me. I promise to do everything towards those ends."

"I do believe I heard that from you before you decided to get ghost. I'm not sure if your cohorts informed you of how Ms. Kathryn works. I don't play games. If that's what you want then bring it and come hard. I don't have time to play games. You want me? Then show me."

No more words were spoken as I took her over and over again that night until she passed out from sheer exhaustion. In the morning when she opened her eyes I repeated the events from the night before until she screamed and begged for me to stop. I continued until she passed out again at which time I left her a note hoping that she would be satisfied until next Thursday.

It was back to work following Thursday but after six months of wining and dining Kathryn I noticed the chill about her beginning to thaw. I asked her for nothing and after a while I would come home to diamond stick pins and other gifts. All these things soon far surpassed the money she owed me and I wanted nothing more than to be free of her.

I'd completed my real estate class and received my certification. Tuesday was so excited by the way I embraced the class and the ease in which I grasped many of the

concepts that she quickly enrolled me in Hunter College on the fast track in pre-law. If it were up to her I'd be taking the bar in no more than five years.

In any case, I was now selling real estate and doing fairly well at it although I hadn't let all my clients go. I still had three or four left but I'd already given them notice. Tuesday was ecstatic and I couldn't have made her more happy than the Saturday I had Thomas pull the car around and we took off for Danbury, Connecticut where Thomas had everything arranged. Tuesday and I were married that morning. After our marriage we spent the following weeks planning to move. We both agreed on Danbury. We had friends up there and had been up on several occasions. I had long ago grown tired of New York and its hectic pace. Connecticut with it 's wide open spaces reminded me a lot more of Georgia and I couldn't wait.

I now had no clients-well that is-aside from Kathryn and it was almost as if she knew that I was about to bail when she informed me that she was pregnant. I'd been around her enough to know when she was telling the truth about something. And she made me escort her to the doctor so happy was she with the news. By this time she'd come to admit that she too was in love and began once more to bury me in lavish gifts.

"Tell me something lover."

"Why is it that you haven't brought up the idea of marriage lately?"

"I saw no reason to. I think you made it quite clear that that wasn't in your plans."

"Perhaps I did give that impression at that time but things change Marcus. We are going to have a baby. And a baby needs two parents in this day and age."

"Not if his father is a Pullman Porter," I smiled.

"Oh stop Marcus. You know I didn't mean that."

"I only wished you'd taken that attitude last month."

"Why last month?"

"Because last month when you told me no I said this is the last time I let this woman reject me. Let me give my love to some one who truly loves me. And so I did. I married Tuesday Frazier."

The look she gave me was terrifying.

"No. you didn't Marcus. I just know you didn't."

"What Kathryn?"

"No, you didn't Marcus. I just know you didn't marry my fuckin' sister to spite me."

"I'm sorry but it's not always about you Kathryn. There is a world aside from yours. I married Tuesday because I love her."

This news so infuriated Kathryn I thought it in my best interest to leave promptly. Revealing my marriage to Kathryn was a bone head move and no sooner than I'd spoken the words I knew it but to see the hurt and anguish on her face made it worth it.

I never mentioned this encounter to Tuesday and wearily awaited the backlash from Kathryn but was surprised when there was none. Perhaps she'd finally come to grips with the fact that our union was God's work and there was little to do now other than to accept it.

Book II

It was close to two months before T and I were even close to resuming normal relations. I felt betrayed that Tuesday hadn't felt it necessary to tell me that a lot of the friction had nothing to do with me but because she and Kathryn were sisters.

"Don't think that it was anything personal Marcus. It's nothing more than a sibling rivalry that's been going on for years. And it's not something I like to readily own up to. Kathryn's been a boon in my side for as long as I can remember. In all, my parents had four girls. Being that I'm the oldest I was held in part responsible for helping to raise them. Kathryn may have been the brightest but there was always something slightly askew when it came to her doing the right thing. She just had a natural tendency to want to do the wrong thing.

My daddy used to call her his little devil. He said that if you took the 'd' off of devil all you have left is evil and that was Kathryn to the core. It was funny when she was a kid but it turned out to be a self-fulfilling prophecy when she got older.

And then for some reason she set her sights on me and decided that if I had it then she had to have it.

And that's not to say that she couldn't very well have had anything she wanted with the beautiful mind she she had but for some reason she felt a need to go about it the wrong way.

I'm telling you Marcus. Kathryn had it all. She literally had the world at her feet. Bright and beautiful I remember her graduating college and coming to New York to stay with me. I'd just gotten married to my first husband James. James and I met about four years earlier when we were in college and now he was one of the first Colored dentists in Harlem. James was a good man, a hard worker and a good provider. But James was a man and was afflicted by temptation.

And of course you know who brought the temptation. Why no other than the devil herself. One day I just happened to come home early to find Kathryn in one of my negligees with James naked, kneeling between her legs."

"Nooo..."

"Oh, but I did. I put them both out but it didn't go away for some quite some time."

"And what did she say?"

"Said I didn't need him. He was no good."

"Somehow I wish she'd just come and told me. Anyway, I divorced James and wished I could have divorced her as well. But that's only one of a thousand transgressions she's committed over the years. Now I just try to be civil and tolerate her."

"Why?"

Tuesday laughed.

"Good question. I ask myself that all the time. But one of the last things my father asked me, God bless his soul, was to look after Kathryn. Now I have three other sisters but the only one he asked me to look after was Kathryn And I have but there's really nothing else I can do. She's chosen the life she wants to lead. And she obviously

is good at robbing, stealing and scamming people. That's her M.O. Now all I can do is keep her at bay and keep a close eye on protecting what is mine."

"And that's why you chose not to share with me that Kathryn was kin to you?"

"Yes. Don't get me wrong. I still love my sister but if I let her close to me she will destroy everything that means something to me. And I refuse to let her destroy the happiness you've brought into my life."

"And now that it's obvious that you have something she wants why haven't we seen any retaliation?"

"Marcus why do you insist on looking a gift in the mouth. Why can't you just be happy to finally have some peace in our lives?"

"Maybe because I've seen her do more for less. This isn't like her."

"You're right but I'm not sleeping on her. I've had twenty four hour surveillance on her for months now."

"And?"

"Believe me whatever's coming will be epic."

"So, you don't believe it's over?"

"It's never over with her. But we can't worry about her Marcus. We close on the house and move on Wednesday. My only other concern is the office. Do you think the hour and a half commute is worth it?"

"With the way sales have been I would say we don't have a choice. We have to stay here in Harlem. We're needed here. If we leave Colored folks will just be taken advantage of and exploited. We, at least offer an alternative to the rents they charge our people. On the other hand, the office is an easy target for Kathryn if she decides to retaliate."

"I was thinking the same thing. I'll put it up on the market tomorrow and see what kind of hits we get. Can't hurt to test the waters."

It was a good move and sound thinking but perhaps our timing was just a little off. At six a.m. the next morning the phone rang.

"Ms. Frazier please."

I handed the phone to Tuesday who was already up. I could tell it wasn't good news when T started rummaging through the junk drawer in the kitchen looking for the stale pack of Newports. I handed her a fresh pack.

"What's wrong baby?"

"Nothing sweetheart. Just another day in the life of Tuesday Frazier."

"You sure?"

"One of our buildings just burned down."

"Oh Lord! Let me guess. The real estate office?"

"Yes. We were just talking about that last night."

"What is they say? The tongue is a sword."

"Yeah. Guess we dragged our feet on that one. How do we stand on the

building?"

"We're good. The insurance will cover the building and I paid little or nothing for it. With the work I put into it and the way it's appreciated over the past ten or fifteen years we stand to be in pretty good shape. It's just that I don't need this right through here."

I could see she was crying and knowing that there was little I could say to comfort her I simply held her in my arms angry once again at Sister Kathryn. Anytime she caused Tuesday pain I bore the heartache. I was tired of feeling this way. Oh, how I wished I could do something. As a boy growing up in Georgia if someone offended you in any manner it was your duty to step to that man or woman and fix it so that it wouldn't again.

I held my baby for a good long time while she leaned into me sobbing on my shoulder as her slender shoulders heaved up and down like two great mountains. And then as if nothing had happened she pulled away from me wiped away the the remaining tears and said.

"Let me get out of here. I have to meet the fire marshal and insurance agent down at the building."

"Do you need me to go?"

"No, bay. But could you call Jen at home and tell her what happened and ask her to reschedule my appointments. If you call her now you may be able to save her from making the trip in."

"I'll do that," I said heading for the phone. Looking out the window of the loft I watched Tuesday walk to the limo where Thomas stood. There wasn't the usual pep in

her step and for the first time since I'd known her she looked worn and old. It was also the first time I'd seen her cry. Her own blood was intentionally killing her.

I called Jen as directed. Kathryn refused to give her a refund when I brought up the disparity in my pay. So, in the name of ethical behavior and professional T and I refunded the young girl's money. Tuesday went even further than that after speaking with the girl in length making her the new receptionist in the Harlem office.

I don't know if T or I liked her more but we were both very fond of her. Jennifer was a pistol but the customers seemed to like her as well. Not long afterward she was promoted to office manager. She was bright and picked up easily. And Tuesday sensing her aptitude for new concepts immediately took her under her wing and began grooming her just as she'd done me in the real estate market.

We'd grown up not far from each other in Marietta and knew many of the same people but that's not what attracted me to her. What I liked most about her was something you didn't readily see in the city. At least I hadn't seen it. She had that fight

in her that came with the good book and arose out of that ol' time religion. I recall the day she asked me to meet her up by the armory on St. Nick.

"Marcus. Good to see you again. You're looking quite well and I guess you're wondering why I asked you to meet me up here today."

"I'm curious."

"You see I was thinking to myself and I said Marcus is a pretty good dude and Lord knows I appreciate what you and Ms. Tuesday have done for me. I think back on the deal I made to sleep with you following my husband's death and I really believe that it didn't work out and the reason I almost lost my money was because I was attempting to do the devil's work. I really believe that. I really believe the Lord rebuked me and taught me a lesson at the same time. And I understand but in that same book it does not allow for people to take advantage and continually abuse you. I know I must have appeared young and dumb, nothing more than a geechie nigga from the swamps of Georgia to Ms. Kathryn. I

must have appeared like fresh bait to Ms. Kathryn when I first got here but what she didn't know was

they got slick and refined miscreants in Georgia too and I peeped her from jump. There were just too

many things that weren't right about her. And whether you and Ms. Tuesday give me back the money

out of general decency or not is not really the issue here. It's the principle. You just can't walk through

life preying on people you think are vulnerable."

I understood. I agreed. So, there was nothing for me to say.

"Well, what do you plan on doing about it?"

It was obvious she'd given it considerable thought.

"Well, at first she made me so angry I was going after her Marietta style and just start wailing on her but

I said no this is not the way to start life in a new place. So, I called my younger brother Miles and told

him. He said he and my other brother Simon

would take care of it but then I thought of the repercussions and didn't want to see any harm come to

you or Ms. Tuesday."s

"Thanks for that Jen," I said knowing that that's not the way Tuesday would want things to happen. She

was adamant about taking the higher road and putting it in the Lord's hands. And Tuesday would have

never wanted to involve Jen and put her at risk. I called her at a little after seven the morning of the fire.

"Morning Jen. Marcus here."

"Morning Marcus. What's up?"

"Nothing good I'm afraid. Looks like the office caught on fire last night. The place was gutted so T had me call you to tell you you had the day off."

"Oh no. Really Marcus? How long before we'll be up and running again?"

"I really don't know. Like I said from what Tuesday tells me the place was gutted."

"Gutted? How's the fire department see it? Are they saying the fire was suspicious? Could it be arson?"

I knew where she was going and wasn't trying to feed her suspicions.

"I don't know. I just got the call a few minutes ago."

"What do you think Marcus?"

"Come on Jen. You know what I think."

"So, let me ask you this Marcus. Why do you continually put up with her shit? She's toxic. She's burned you. She's burned me. She burns everyone she comes in contact with. She has no boundaries or parameters. Anyone that would set fire to her own sister's property has some very serious issues that need to be addressed and they need to be addressed now."

"I agree with you wholeheartedly. You know we come from the same place Jen."

"Yes, we do. So, you and I both know that in Marietta this comes down to a good old time ass kicking. In Marietta it comes down to that good ol' time religion that says an eye-for-an-eye."

"I hear you but I gave my word to Tuesday."

"Well, I didn't. This bitch already stole from me and somehow got a pass. Now she's burnt my place of business to the ground and put me out of work. And I wasn't even her target. But this is the last time I'm going to let her fuck with any of us. Let me go Marcus. I've got shit to do."

After she hung up I was worried. I knew she was frustrated and distraught. I just didn't know to what degree.

With the building gone Jennifer found herself once again in a familiar place, unemployed and penniless. And who was responsible? No one other than that damn Kathryn. At least that's where all fingers pointed.

"Miles."

"Hey Jen. How's my favorite sister?"

"I wish I could say everything's good but I'd be lying," Jennifer replied before recounting her plight with Kathryn.

"Okay sweetheart. Let me get in touch with Simon. Call me back with her address and we'll take care of it. Minutes later she called back.

"We'll take care of it tonight."

"Don't kill her."

"Come on sis. That kinda talk isn't necessary. This is me. You know we're not killas. I'm just tryin' to stop this bitch from hurting you anymore baby girl."

At eight fifteen that evening three men in their early to mid-twenties crouched behind the blue Crown Victoria parked at the curb. They were waiting. The busy

 avenue was uncommonly quiet when the black limo pulled up across the street. A handsome woman in her mid to late thirties exited the limo and made her way to the door of the brownstone. Dressed in a charcoal gray business suit she had no idea what hit her when the three men approached her guns drawn. Clearly shaken she offered no resistance.

Opening the door to the brownstone the three men moved inside and made quick work in ransacking the home. The burglars was reported to have made off with over ten thousand dollars in jewelry alone although those that knew the victim said it was probably closer to five grand.

In the end, the police report reported some minor facial lacerations and a sprained wrist. Still, and although the men were unmasked the woman was unable or unwilling to give the police a description. Like Jennifer the woman had her own way of dispensing out justice.

The news circulated quickly about one of Harlem's leading citizens being accosted. The colored churches were horrified as well and rallied their congregations to put pressure on their councilmen for some relief from these atrocities. Petitions were filled out and signed calling for the city to provide better policing and community watches.

At the Breath of Life Church in Christ where the woman regularly attended and was a highly regarded member special prayers were offered for her speedy recovery. The Sisters of Charity the women's group founded and headed by victim collected close to three thousand dollars on her behalf. And as of yet there still hadn't been a peep from the victim. Oh, she talked to the sisters who came to visit her while she was in the hospital to share their condolences, stories and sweet potato pies but not even to her most trusted confidantes did she share with the unpleasantries of that night.

The Sunday following Pastor Dunn's preaching an announcement was made.

"Brothers and sisters as I'm sure you've heard one of our stronger church members and community leaders was assaulted at her home last week. She's spent the past week in ICU at St. Luke's. She was released this morning and insisted on making this her first stop. Sisters and brothers may I introduce to you one of the leading ladies of the Breath of Life Church in Christ, Sister Kathryn.

The crowd broke into a huge cheer as she was wheeled into the room.

"Thank you. Thank you I would really like to thank all of you who came to visit me and said prayers on my behalf and sent cakes and pies that added twenty pounds to each hip. But I am not here to talk about the heinous crime committed against me. This was only the good Lord's way of seizing the opportunity to protect his flock. I had no idea how often this type of crime happens in our neighborhoods but it happens more often times than not and far too often.

It's not a new occurrence and we have asked the city on more than one occasion to provide us more patrols. And they have done little to nothing so it is up to us to provide our own security and our own protection. We have the right to walk freely through our own communities. What I am suggesting is that we begin policing our own neighborhood to insure our safety. And I would like to begin today. So, if any of you would like to sign up there are people in the rear of the church that will take your contact information. We are also having a meeting tomorrow to discuss any questions or concerns concerning the greater Christian Community Watch.

For those of you who do not know me. My name is Sister Kathryn.

From the sound of the applause it was abundantly aware that she'd hit a nerve. And it was even more apparent the following night when close to two hundred people showed up at the church's lecture hall to discuss the increasing assaults and mugging in the neighborhood.

"Good evening ladies and gentleman. The reason we have gathered here tonight is to come together and address the ever-growing violence in our neighborhood. This violence against women and the elderly by thugs has got to stop! And if we can not count on law enforcement who our tax dollars pay to protect us then we must do it ourselves. I have therefore had my assistants take your contact information and place you in groups of four. Your job is not to confront anyone even if we should see a crime in progress. Our job is simply to let our presence be felt. What we are essentially is a deterrent. Our

presence should if nothing else stop these cowards from preying on the weak and infirmed.

We will also be offering a series of classes on self-defense. The classes are free and all are welcomed me to join. Training for the Christian Community Watch will begin this Wednesday and will run Mondays, Wednesdays, and Fridays for a month. At which the time you will receive your certification and will then be assigned your post.

We will also be setting up a special team which for now will simply be called the team of eight. This select or special team will be made of veterans, and former law enforcement personnel and will be attached to our elderly and higher crime pockets in our neighborhoods.

Now let's take a few minutes to get to know each other. Some of the good sisters of the church have provided some refreshments for you to enjoy. So if there aren't any question I will join you in the lobby.

Sister Kathryn was all smiles in the lobby as people approached questioning the true intent of the program. She fielded all as best she could. And when she couldn't she simply said.

"I do believe that's something we'll have to look into that further," before scribbling it down on her yellow legal pad.

There was a man, a tall man who looked over the crowd. His sights were set on the polished little lady in the blue, floral dress. When she finished making her rounds he eased his way over to her.

"Sister Kathryn. My name is Hank Whitted and I was listening to your call for volunteers."

"Nice to meet you, " the tiny woman said something as she stared up at the mountain of a man who stood before her. He was quite handsome she had to admit. "What is it that I can help you with?"

"Well, I was hoping that I might be able to help you."

"Do we have your contact info?"

"Yes."

"Then if you check the lists I'm sure you will find one that corresponds with where you reside."

The big man smiled.

"I don't think you understand. I was curious as to your elite group. Have you assembled them yet?"

"No. That's still in the planning stages."

"Perhaps I can help you with that. I've just returned from overseas where I spent the last three years providing security as part of the military police. A few of my buddies have come to the ends of their tours and decided to continue providing security stateside. We would like to volunteer our services to you at no cost."

"At no cost? Okay. Mr. Whitted what's in it for you?"

The large man smiled.

"I assure you ma'am. We don't want anything. Most of us live right here in the

community. Many of us have families and want the same things for their families and that's safety and

security."

"Do you have a family Mr. Whitted?"

"No. At least not yet. I hope to one day though. I'm still laying the groundwork. There are still some

things I'd like to establish before taking on the responsibility of a wife and kids."

"Such as?"

"Well, I just bought a little three bedroom out in St. Albans. Now my focus is to get our security

company up and running. We've done the paperwork and filed the necessary forms with the city. Now

we're just waiting for the word to spread about our services."

"And this is free promotion. It's an interesting concept you're promoting though. An all-colored

security company? Woo! That's a hoot," she laughed. "And who's brainchild was this if you don't mind

me asking? Please tell me what white man is going to put his fortune in the hands of some colored

boys? That's like asking the rat to guard the cheese factory or the wolf to guard the hen house," she

said laughing again.

"You're absolutely right and that's why I'm offering you our services to your organization at no cost. It's

not only an opportunity for us to showcase our talents but

allow the world to see colored folks in a new light."

"And who are you?"

"We are a really well disciplined unit of former military police that have studied and are well-versed in the art of war. Our mission stateside is basically the same as it was overseas. Only overseas we were responsible for protecting Uncle Sam's interests. The only difference now is our focus. Our goal is no longer to protect Uncle Sam's interests but our own. We want to help build strong, independent, self-sufficient communities that are for us and by us. And when we need both need help and protection we don't have to turn and look for outside help and be at the mercy of the police who look at us like second class citizens. Instead we can turn to A Thousand Brothers. By the time we are finished building we will have an army. We will have the first army built to protect and serve the Negro."

"Pretty lofty goals I must say Mr.Whitted and you do sound passionate. Tell me. How many men do you have in your employ presently?"

"So far we have seven in the New York City area but we will have our first graduating class by the end of the month bringing our numbers to twenty."

"Sounds good Mr. Whitted but I do have some suggestions. I think one of the ways in which we'll be a little more easily accepted is to portray ourselves as God's Christian soldiers. I really think that A Thousand Brothers armed by the United States might be considered a threat by most white folks."

"You're right sister. But even with the threat of other young brothers running around the streets robbing and muggin' they still don't pose the threat that America does. You know I just spent three years in Uncle Sam's army. I had the opportunity to visit

both France and Italy and in neither country did I even remotely experience the racism that goes on right here at home. We have been pacifists far too long. If we can fight to defend America's freedom then we must find it in us to defend our own."

"You seem quite passionate and that's something we need more of. We need our young men to be more passionate, more driven concerning our cause as a people so I applaud you but more importantly I need local protection for our people. Can your organization provide that?"

"I do believe we can. Now would you agree to dinner with me so we can work out the nuances of our partnership?"

The woman had to smile at the request. She was still taking in the rather formidable figure when he rose and extended his hand.

"I'll pick you up at eight," he smiled.

"Let me give you my address."

"No need for that?" The woman looked puzzled.

"Did you forget that I am a head of security?"

Book II

Jennifer couldn't remember ever being so angry. She'd left her mama teary-eyed to follow her

childhood sweetheart Bradley Jenkins to New York City. They had had a plan. Bradley was going to do

two years in the Army send his money home to Jen who was a financial wizard when it came to their

finances. They had a plan and they were building their future now. Life was good. And then the war had

taken Bradley like it had so many other Colored boys around this time.

The women of The Breath of Life Church in Christ had been there for her after Bradley's death. They'd

helped her through the grieving process and she'd grown strong again until she believed she could stand

on her own again. And then just when she was ready to try again someone had referred her to Sister

Kathryn who had her own Class on Closure. And why not trust Sister Kathryn? She was well respected

within the church and everyone else in the church had been so supportive. And though Sister Kathryn

had swindled her and she had considered blowing the whistle it was Marcus and Tuesday who had made

it alright in the end.

This whole Christian Community Watch had taken off perhaps just a little quicker than the good sister

had hoped but she would have never expected the turn out at the church being so large. She was still

not feeling herself and her first day out of hospital had been nothing less than overwhelming.

Perhaps this is where she should have concerned herself all along. The community had needs that far

out-weighed the churches and there seemed a limitless amount of souls with a myriad of problems. If only she'd been a man she could have been an alderman or city councilman and traded policies for bids and favors.

And if it that hadn't been enough for one day she'd had the occasion to meet that adorable, hunk who called himself Hank Whitted. In a manner of minutes this tall, dark, muscular, stranger had introduced, himself, come under her employ and had her preparing for a date that very night despite her facial bruises. He was smooth, well spoken and damn he was handsome. He had goals, goals not to far from hers and with just the right bit of persuasiveness there was a slight chance that she may be able to coerce him to do her bidding. But that was for later.

Tonight she had a date.

Dressed in an all black chiffon dress that hugged every inch of her she sat legs crossed in the sitting room. If she wasn't so sore from the beating she'd taken she'd insist on there staying in. Still, she needn't be so forward. If he were like every other man she knew he'd fall into her clutches within a week and be begging to serve her in anyway she desired.

He appeared at her door in a park charcoal gray suit that spelled money.

"Sister."

"Mr. Whitted," she said wondering if staying in might be just be what the doctor ordered before grabbing her shawl.

"I have a car waiting,"

The night was everything she could have expected. And she had everything she could do not to invite him in. Yet, there was something that wasn't quite right. Sure, he'd been the perfect gentlemen and his choice of wines showed he was cultured but there was something not exactly right about it. She'd desired him more than anyone she'd known but he hadn't shown his desire towards her the way men do and that bothered her.

She 'd been flirtatious and he'd not responded. Instead he kept the conversation light when it wasn't on business.

"You know if your men are as well trained as you say they are there may be other opportunities available. Other opportunities that may prove rather lucrative."

Smiling and dropping his head the tall man paused.

"Sorry, ma'am. Perhaps I didn't make myself clear. And by no means do I mean to sound un appreciative but we are more concerned with the upliftment of us as a people than just the monetary gain."

"And I feel exactly the same way. I've spent almost half my life helping to uplift my people and money, more than you may realize is needed to do that. So, I've learned to always leave bridges and avenues open. You may consider that an option."

"I might at that."

The two developed an almost unbreakable and undeniable bond over the next two or three months. The Christian Community Watch was now up and in full swing and everyone from the pastor to the mayor was applauding the efforts.

And when street thugs and local gangs became obstinate about keeping, their turf. The Elite Eight who had now turned into the Elite Twelve and was now The Elite Sixteen would be called in and the problem eliminated. No one asked how or questioned their methods. They simple applauded.

One evening after sitting around discussing the day's events in her office on Edgecombe Avenue she turned and looked him squarely in the eye.

"You know Hank, we've been through a lot these last three or four months."

"That we have."

"And I have to admit I am curious as to one thing. I mean I understand that you're focused and driven but there's still one thing that perplexes me."

"And what's that?"

"Well, the whole time we've spent together you've never approached me."

The large man put his head down. He seemed to be in deep thought.

"Hank."

"Was just thinking is all. You know when I was younger women like you would never have given me the time of day so I worked on bettering myself. Now I don't worry about women. I'm just concentrated on bettering myself. I might think about including them in my life if I ever get close to realizing who it is I am and what I want out of life but until then I guess I just don't have the time."

"That's interesting."

"You see there's no rush for me to be in a relationship. I have other more important things to be doing. When we started I was responsible for seven men. Now I have forty-two men depending on me for their training and livelihood. Even if I found that woman I have other allegiances."

"That's really interesting but you know what they say about all work and no play."

"I've always been a rather dull boy but let me ask this. What do you propose I do?"

"Perhaps I can show you better than I can tell you."

"Perhaps you can but it won't be tonight. I've got twenty soldiers ready to deploy to Baltimore in the morning and a graduating class at noon."

Then without another word the tall man rose grabbing his hat and overcoat walked out.

Oh, that man. Oh, how he annoyed her. He was the real reason for her newfound success and she was basking in the glory. Small towns and cities throughout the country were now demanding Hank's Elite Services. Business had grown exponentially and even though she had yet found a way to the proceeds she knew she had a gold mine in Hank and for the first time in her life she really didn't give a damn about the money. She just liked being along for the ride. And his rejection only solidified the fact that she had to have him and would. What he didn't know is she had all intentions on marrying him?

The two met every morning at nine a.m. to go over the day's itinerary and every evening to discuss any news or concerns before the night watch went out on patrol. They were now in Philadelphia, Boston and tomorrow they were expanding to Baltimore. He would be driving down, leaving her for a week or two until were firmly established before returning home. That's the way things were right up until today.

That morning before he stopped by the office before he hit the road.

"Morning."

"Morning sweetheart. Would you please take my luggage to the car for me?"

All six feet nine inches of Hank Whitted stood there. Feet glued to the floor he knew she couldn't be serious. They'd just gone through this whole thing the night before but she would not be denied.

"Hank. Are you paying attention? Hank to earth. Would you please put my luggage in the car?"

"And where do you think you're going?"

"Why I'm going with you sweetheart. After all my name is on the front lines. I think that I should at least be able to see what type of image it is that I'm supposedly portraying."

"I solely agree by why the sudden change of heart? Just a week or two ago when I invited you to the Boston opening you had something else to do and to this date you hardly seem interested so why all of a sudden the sudden interest in the Baltimore project? Come on sister. What's really going on here?"

"Nothing's going on. Why are you always so suspicious? Why can't it be just what it is?"

"Because most people say one thing and mean another. The world is full of people with ulterior motives."

"Well, I don't fall in that stereotype. It's just like I told you sweetheart I just need to see and make sure the program is adhering to the guidelines we set up."

"And that's it?"

"Well, I do have to admit I may have some ulterior motives as well," she said winking at him. You see this time away will give me a chance to get to know you better."

"And you can't do that here?"

"I don't know if you've noticed or not but I've been trying. It's been rather slow going up 'til now but I have another idea if you'd just put my luggage in the car Mr. Whitted."

The tall man smiled.

"I'll put them in the car but I promise you you're going to be quite disappointed. I'll be working twelve to sixteen hour days and by I finally get back to the room it's lights out. After work there's little time for anything else."

"Enough talk Hank. Are you ready to go?"

The tall man loaded the luggage before lighting a cigarette and leaning on the fender of the car. She would definitely be in the way but she was stubborn and there was no way of convincing her otherwise. He had no other choice than to oblige her wishes and let her come along. He knew where her intentions lay and it had nothing to do with providing a protection and security to anyone other than herself. The needs of Colored folks never entered her mind. Her needs were her own although she was convinced by this time that she would make her needs his.

He, on the other hand, seeing her for who she really was avoided everything but the mission at hand when it came to her. For the mot self-taught he'd learned most things the hard way. There was little difference when it came to women. She was like so many he'd come across who were blessed with an abundance of good looks and a lack of anything tangible to parlay into a meaningful relationship if he were interested. She like a lot of them he'd run into lately were simply trying to parlay their looks into maneuvering a man into their clutches and making him responsible for their welfare. He'd avoided it thus far and despite her desperate measures he would avoid her as well.

The partnership between the two had worked well thus far and she'd been right. Naming it the Christian Community Watch was genius. Colored folks were facing many of the same problems across the nation. Calls were now coming in from everywhere. It was almost impossible to keep up although he felt well rewarded for his efforts.

She was now beginning to see dollar signs despite professing her love for the tall man. It was hard to avoid the steady phone calls bidding for Hank's services. But as of yet she had received nothing other than a rather nominal finders fee for referring the business to Hank. But she was convinced that after this trip all that would be ancient history. After all, the idea itself had been hers and it was a good partnership and they got along well. He was bright and driven with a well placed plan in place whether he was Christian Community Watch was growing exponentially with the tall man at the helm.

"Are we almost there sweetheart?"

"Another half hour or so."

When they arrived at the front desk hank confirmed his reservation.

"I'm also going to need a room for my friend."

"Oh, don't be silly, sweetheart. Why waste the money? One room will be fine ma'am."

The tall man was really taken back by this sudden change in plans.

"Listen. Can you have a bottle of Jameson's sent to the room?"

"No problem Mr. Whitted. I'll do that now," she said picking up the phone.

The woman seemed tickled by this latest news.

"I guess Johnny's does take a little time for rest and relaxation after all. I was hoping he did."

Ignoring the remark Hank carried the woman's luggage to the room. He couldn't remember seeing her

happier but he had things to tend to.

"Oh, look hon. There's a complimentary bottle of wine on the bed and a basket of fruit. Oh, this is nice.

Would you like a glass of wine to help you relax after that drive?"

"No, thanks. I'm going to grab a quick shower. I have a meeting at one and it's already after twelve."

"Baby. Why don't you just send Charlie Earl in your place. You've really got to learn to delegate."

"I have a tendency to believe that I am my own best representative. I'd feel better if I was at the initial

meeting with the pastors so I can get a feel for what they are looking for."

The small woman ignored the big man and turned on the shower for her man before pouring him a glass

of Jameson's and slipping on a most revealing red gown exposing all but the nipples of her breasts.

Sipping the wine she listened until she no longer heard the shower before entering the bathroom.

It was the first time she'd taken such liberties with this mountain of a man and immediately had second thoughts when she saw the enormity of the man. She gasped before resigning herself to the idea that she would be in time able to accommodate him.

Ignoring the woman in front of him Hank had other thoughts on his mind. Sitting to dress Hank was a thousand miles away. Colored folks were scared. That was one of im gone.the reasons he'd been summoned. He'd rehearsed his delivery countless times and he had to remember, to constantly remind himself not to come across as a nationalist passionate about uplifting Colored folk. No. He couldn't do that. Colored folks were scared.

The woman found the baby oil and began massaging the big man's shoulders.

"Does that feel good baby?"

Nodding he continued getting addressed.

"Just give me five minutes baby. Let me rinse some of this road dust off of me and I'll finish your massage. You never know. I may have a surprise in store for you. I'll be out in five," she said winking at the tall man before letting the dress fall to the floor exposing herself to him. There. That should do it she thought before stepping in the shower and pulling the curtain closed. She smiled. But when she got out she found him gone.

"Damn that man," she screamed in frustration. She screamed at everyone and at no one. Why was he continually rejecting her? Why was he constantly telling her no?

The days that followed were almost identical and each time she tried to corral him he would escape her. By the time they were ready to leave the tiny woman was fit to be tied.

"Sweetheart. We've been here close to a week and you have shown little or no interests in my wants and needs. You even chose the couch over the bed. What is it? Are you not attracted to me?"

"We had this same conversation in New York. I told you this was a business trip. I told you my only concern was trying to establish my business. And you know what you did? You ignored all that," he said smiling, "The only thing that was important to you was what you had on your itinerary. You see. You had your own agenda and weren't concerned with mine."

"That's not true Hank. My success are and failure are both dependent on you. It's just that it's always business with you. Why can't you find a little time for me. You have to know how I feel about you man."

The huge mountain of a man dropped his head. It was obvious he was in deep thought. He was too close to this woman already. His interests were not hers. She had no knowledge of security and wasn't interested in learning. What she did enjoy was the fan fair it brought her and now she was interested. in how she could make his work profitable for her. He knew her type. She was for lack of a better word a gold digger content to make her hers off the labors of others.

"What if I had the time to give you little lady? What would you do with it?"

"How long do I have?"

"Well, we're supposed to be back in New York by twelve. You know we have that meeting with the pastors from East New York?"

"Then I'm going to need for you to hush and follow my lead," she said as she began to slowly massage every inch of the large mountain of a man. When she'd aroused him enough she invited him to enter her. Gasping she reached for anything to hold onto. My God. He was huge.

She screamed with each thrust until she was hoarse and no screams came out. It hadn't taken that long to adjust to his length and thickness but his stamina was another story in itself. For more than an hour he went at her sometimes loving her casually, gently before ravaging her every orifice before drilling her into unconsciousness. She lost count of how many times she came in his arms and at his command. And then she passed out. When she woke up he was still plunging the length of his shaft into her. The steady pounding aroused her once more and she met his thrusts before passing out again. When she finally woke up she was singing a different tune.

"Baby. With me as your woman helping to guide you we can rise to the top in no time. I can supply the capital you need to really expand. With me behind you we can expand nationally in no time."

"Why are you bringing this up now?"

"Well, that was my objective when I came down here. There were things I wanted to see before I invested in you and the company. I do believe both of those questions have been answered. I'm not usually this forward but I want you to be my man. I want to be your woman."

"Come on woman. With everything going on right through here you know that would never work."

"Baby. We are going to make a fortune. Do you hear me? A fortune! And I don't think we could have made it this far without each other. The resounding success of the Community Watch is testimony to our working so well together. We're compatible.Can't you see that we are equally yoked? And on top of that I like the way you make me feel," she said pulling the huge man back to bed.

Several weeks later little had changed. Her office took the calls for the Christian Community Watch and when her secretary and receptionist both started lobbying for someone to just answer the Watch's calls she grew angry.

"Hello. Hank sweetheart. Listen. Are you busy this evening? Oh, you are. Okay well make time one evening this week. I need to discuss some things with you. Strictly business but make it soon."

They met the next evening at her home.

"Hank. I want you to understand one thing and one thing only. I am angry."

"And why would that be?"

"Okay. Let's put Baltimore aside. That may have been a mistake on my part. I may have seen and wanted things not possible and in so doing mixed business with pleasure. I'll own that and that's not my concern today. I thought we had a partnership but as of yet I have yet to see any financial consideration. I know you're making money hand over fist because yesterday both my receptionist and secretary came to tell be about the influx of calls and ask me to hire more staff just to handle the calls. Now from what I've come to to understand is that you charge communities more than ten thousand a week to go in and clean up and to train. And as of this date I do not believe the Sisters of Charity have received a plug nickel."

"Is this what this is really all about it?"

"Yes my love this is what this is all about it but I'm gonna give you a pass on the fact that you're exploiting us if I can get you to do a few local jobs for me."

"And you keep the profits from these jobs?"

"I think that's fair."

"You'll have to give me some time on this. I would hate to commit and then not be able to come through. Don't want to overextend myself. You understand. I'm sure."

"I suppose I do but just to be on the safe side I'm gonna need some show of good faith from you."

The big man knew assuming to know what she was alluding to picked her up and carried her up the stairs. She giggled and tried to extricate herself from the large man's

grasp before he ravaged her and left her laying on her bed unconscious and still half dressed. It hadn't lasted long at all this time but in the fifteen minutes or so it had she'd cried, screamed and begged him to marry her with the morning light.

The following day after their morning meeting she had difficulty looking at him.

"How are you this morning beautiful?"

"I'm fine and you?" she said still refusing to make eye contact.

"You know I've never been proposed to before," he said teasing.

"Oh, Mr. Whitted. You are so crass," she said before grabbing her jacket and pocketbook. "I never want to see or hear from you again. Never."

"Does that mean I won't be seeing or hearing from you tonight? And to think I was really starting to feel you," he laughed on his way out the door.

He hoped that that would be the end of it, the end of her, the end of her lies and insincerity but hardly a day passed when he received a call.

"Hank," she screamed. "I found him. My driver's sitting in front of his house as we speak."

She was screaming with excitement and he could barely discern what she was saying.

"Whoa! Slow down. Take a deep breath and slow down. Okay now slow down and tell me what you're talking about."

"I saw the man that mugged me. I saw him when I was down on 8th Avenue visiting a friend so I had Thomas follow him home. We sat there and then he brought me home so I could call you. I'm telling you I saw him."

"Are you absolutely sure? You know these are very serious accusations you're making?"

"Yes. I'm sure. I'm positive. My driver's sitting in front of his house as we speak."

"Okay. Tell your driver to get the address and get out of there. We don't know what type of people we're dealing with and we don't want them to get suspicious and him to get hurt. Call me back once you do that."

No sooner than he hung up than the phone rang.

"Okay. My team's mobilized. We're going to shoot up there just as soon as they get here. How do you want us to handle it?"

"I want their asses beaten just like they did me. I want them to know that we are not afraid to stand up to them." She was screaming again.

"Okay. Okay. Calm down. We'll pick you up in a few minutes. Be ready."

"I'm always ready baby. You already know that."

After notifying his team of the changes the rather large man hailed a cab and after picking her up made for the address she'd given him. Two groups of men stood at

opposite ends of the street in all black. Most of the folks in the community had grown accustomed to seeing these groups of men from time to time and felt a little safer just for having them there. There were four men in each group and upon seeing their leader they converged on him.

"There's been no movement since we got here but we're keeping a close eye. How do you want to do this?" team leader Charlie Earl asked.

"There's a back door that's shaky at best and a fire escape leading to two second floor windows. The windows are open. To tell you the truth Hank we could have had this all cleared up and been back in the bed in all the time it took you to get here. i though we we were a mobile unit? Ready at all times. I never knew any of us to be slowed down by a skirt," Doc, his second in command said teasingly but still with some truth in it.

Hank shot a glance over to her.

"I've been trying to tell my friend that but she seems to think that she's the exception."

"And of course you told her nothing comes before the welfare of the nation."

"I did Doc."

"Just want to make that clear. Anywhere there's the back door, upstairs and of course there's always the front door."

"Sounds good and you say there's only perp inside?"

"Appears that way."

"Okay. We're going to hit all three. I have ten minutes to six. I need everyone to synchronize their watches. Doc, I want you to take one team and hit the back door. Charlie I need you to go in through the second floor and the lady and I will pretend to be Jehovah Witnesses and attempt to enter through the front door."

The men quickly dispersed and got into their positions. At six o'clock sharp there appeared a small commotion at the rear of the house. The woman's knocks had gone virtually unnoticed but moments later Charlie Earl's smiling face appeared at the door.

"Welcome to my humble abode. The owner who I assume you are here to see is temporarily incapacitated. Come in."

"What's up man?" the young man shouted. "Why y'all up in my house? I don't what the fuck is wrong but y'all definitely got the wrong house."

Before the young man could utter another word he was hit flush on the cheek with the butt of the .45. The swelling was immediate.

"I'm sorry sir but if there's anything I need to know I'll do the asking. Other than that you are to keep your mouth shut. Is that understood?" Charlie Earl asked the man now holding his face. "Now what is your name son?"

"My name is Miles?"

"And what is it that you do Miles?"

"I'm a short order cook at Nathan's Times Square."

"And that's all you do Miles?"

"Yes sir."

"That's interesting. It must be hard trying to maintain this apartment on a Nathan's salary."

"Yes sir. I mean you're right. My brother and a roommate also live here and help out on the rent. Why are we late on the rent or something. I don't know. I just give my portion to my brother on the first of the month. He takes care of all that."

"So, where are you brother and roommate?"

"They should be home in about ten or fifteen minutes," he said glancing at his watch. "That's who I thought you were. Can I ask you a question?"

No sooner had those very words rolled off his tongue that the heavy thud of steel against flesh were heard for a second time that evening. From the sound of it I had a feeling any future comments would be heavily weighed.

"Something tells me you're having a little difficulty with the concept of only speaking when spoken to but let's try again. Do you remember this woman?" Doc asked the frightened boy.

"I ain't never seen her in my life."

"So, what you're trying to tell me is that you, your brother and your friend didn't assault this woman outside her home on Edgecombe before taking her inside and burglarizing her home? That's what you're trying to tell me?"

There was no need to continue. The young man's eyes said it all.

"She robbed my sister of a thousand dollars and then burned her place of employment to the ground. My sister just wanted her to know that you can't treat people like that, like their less than you just because you have a little money and prestige. That's not the way we was brought up. If someone hits you then you hit 'em back."

"You may be right youngblood but even if what you say is true I don't think three grown men beating a woman is the way to get your message across."

Hank dismissed everyone but Doc who was nearly his size and had a pretty even demeanor. Only the five men remained. All three boys recounted the same story of the woman robbing their sister before burning down her place of business.

"What's your sister's name?"

"Jennifer," the younger of the two brothers volunteered.

"And where does Jennifer live?"

"Don't tell 'em Miles. Don't tell 'em," Simon shouted before being punched in the face breaking his nose and sending blood spurting everywhere.

"Unlike you Simon I don't make it a habit of punching and beating up on defenseless women. What I am trying to confirm is if what you're telling me is true. I can't afford to be in business with Colored folks whose intentions are to rob other Colored folks who are out here struggling to make it. What you three have told me is not good and before I take any more action I need to get to the bottom of this. Now what is her address?"

The boys provided the necessary information.

"I will see all three of you tomorrow night at the armory up on St. Nick. And I would like to thank all three of you in advance for volunteering for the Christian Community Watch. If anyone should have any problems just tell them that Hank sent you and you are to start training immediately. I don't know if you know it or not but you three have been the inspiration for all of us," he said pointing to nine men dressed in black outside of the apartment. And then as if nothing at all had taken place the tall man turned and left.

"Oh, thank you so much darling. Your team is so professional. I was so impressed though I didn't know you carried guns. You were like men among boys."

"The pain of war, the killing will take the boyhood innocence right outta you," Doc said overhearing the conversation.

"The guns are just there as a deterrent," Hank replied. Our people know that you're carrying a gun there's less resistance overall. To date we have never even had to show a gun."

"Thank God! Say Hank you must be a little rattled after that. Why don't you come in and have a nightcap with me? I think I may have still have some of that Jameson's left."

"I don't know. You know what happened the last time I had some Jameson's."

"Exactly what I was counting on," she smiled.

"You're absolutely sure now? The last time I drank Jameson's al I heard was, 'Is that all you got daddy'. Your ass was on crutches for two weeks. When the doctor finally took you off of them and I asked if you were alright you told me you thought I'd missed a spot and maybe I should come back and revisit it til I got it right. That's the day I realized you were looney and you may be a threat to yourself," the huge

man said laughing.

"Oh, shut up Hank," the woman laughed. "Maybe we shouldn't go to that extreme. Perhaps you could

just touch it up for me."

"I might could," he said grinning back.

When the knock came it was hardly a surprise. She'd gone over to prepare Sunday dinner the same way she did every Sunday after church only to find her brothers beaten just well enough so they'd gotten the message so when the knock came she expected it.

Name's Hank. Hank Whitted. I'm sure your brothers told you about me. I'm in business with Kathryn and I'd like to think that I was on the side of the Lord in protecting His sheep but after what your brothers told me I'm not so sure so I was hoping that you could tell me exactly what happened so I could get to the bottom of it."

"It's all true Mr. Whitted and the funny thing is that in the burning of the office I wasn't even the intended target. I'm just what you might call collateral damage. But seriously Mr. Whitted my brothers have no reason to lie."

"I don't doubt that they are good boys if not a little misguided," he said wiking at her. But like I said I'd like to hear it straight from the horse's mouth."

Several times during her telling Hank what Sister Kathryn had done to her the young woman broke down in tears.

"Understand Mr. Whitted that I am merely trying to carve a niche for myself and it seems like other people's intent is to wait for some unexpecting victim to pass by so they fleece them of everything they have. She's a thief. She's like a scavenger who's just waiting for someone to prey on. That's who she is. That's what she does. And now thanks to her she's had my brothers beaten up."

"I'm terribly sorry about that but I think they'll be better men because of it. I was always brought up to respect women. I don't care what they've done you do not put your hands on them. Now that they know that they've signed up to be a part of my organization and will serve and protect those that cannot protect themselves. So, they'll be fine. But let me look into these allegations. I'll let you know what we come up with by the end of the week."

She nodded as the tall man stood taking her hand in his and shaking it before heading to the door. She then picked up the phone.

After the meeting with Mr. Whitted Jen picked up the phone and called Marcus. The two friends agreed to meet later that afternoon.

Marcus and Tuesday loved the little, three bedroom Tudor style house. It was modest by all accounts but it was more than enough for them. Tuesday had even gone so far as to take off two weeks just to decorate. She spent her days at Pier 1 and Tuesday Mornings and she was if nothing else happy.

Marcus remained steadfast at work. he was now out selling Tuesday and the commissions were mounting. At twenty seven he had quite an impressive portfolio. Tuesday guided him in the procurement of properties that had a quick turnover value and his passion only increased.

The Jews who owned most of the real estate in Harlem were now selling choice bits of real estate in Harlem for far below market value because of the recent and sudden influx of Southern Negroes following the war. Marcus and Tuesday tried to grab it all. Despite all attempts at white flight many white landowners refused to sell to Negro. Tuesday remained unfazed and refused to be turned away recruiting Melissa's help to set up a dummy corporation with Melissa as the front man. She then had Melissa contact her father who in turn contacted the mayor concerning some low end properties opening up that could be used as subsidized housing. Tuesday sold a few of these. Most of the ones she sold required too much maintenance and work to be truly profitable. But even these she doubled and tripled her monies. It was brilliant. It increased the amount of inexpensive housing by ten fold and let the city do the maintenance and upkeep. And with her keeping a twenty percent interest she would always have a check coming in.

Yes. Life was good and perhaps the best news was that they hadn't heard from Kathryn.

It could be worse.

Perhaps Jen was right in her assessment of how to deal with her. I guess it was just a case of standing up to the bully and making the bully atone for his transgressions. After a month or so he convinced Tuesday that an office in Sugar Hill was essential for their continual growth. And so with Jen's help they set up a new office just blocks away from the old office. only this time the office was provided with twenty four hour security. And so far there had been no problems. But something was wrong. If this was business Jen would have contacted Tuesday. She always did. That was just out of respect. But when she contacted it was usually over or concerning our problem child.

The Chock-Ful-of-Nuts downtown was one of my favorite eateries and sometimes I'd get the hankering and no matter where I was I would stop and head to one for a chicken salad sandwich, a cup of black coffee and a slice of lemon meringue pie. Those were their specialties and I would travel miles of the way to have them. Today I did not want to go. But here I was when Jennifer walked up.

"Long time no see," I smiled.

"Yeah. Give a little colored boy from Georgia a few dollars and he forgets everything," Jen responded. "In case you forgot they call me Jen."

"Ahhh... You know it's not like that. I've just been working. In fact that's all I do is work. But enough about me. I heard you bought a cute little three bedroom out in Queens. Heard it was a steal. You going to keep it or you gonna flip it?"

"Whoa! Slow down Marcus. Yes. I bought a home thanks to your wife's help and I've barely unpacked so it's way too soon to ask what I intend to do with it."

"Heard you're just about to graduate and join our team."

"Yes. And I am so excited. I graduate a week from Thursday."

"Are you ready?"

"Not to sound arrogant but I don't think I could be more ready. I mean between managing the office with Ms. Tuesday always in my ear how could I be anything but ready?' Jen smiled.

"Well, that's good. Now tell me what brings you here today?" He already knew it had something to do with Kathryn but despite his pledge to his wife he was tired of her intrusion into their life. He had had enough. This time he would do it his way and that would not be a good thing for anyone involved.

Jennifer told him the story of her brothers and the large man that had stopped by to talk to to her. Before she'd finished Marcus hugged her then turned and walked away. She didn't know but Marcus had had enough.

Hailing the first cab uptown he headed home. He'd talked to Tuesday about this whole so-called sibling rivalry that had people looking over their shoulders, ducking bullets and knocking people out of work and was unable to see how Tuesday was handling it. But that is what she said wasn't it? 'Just let me handle it.' And yet unbeknownst to Tuesday three more people had been assaulted thanks to Kathryn.

It almost seemed inevitable. It was up to him being the only man of any significance involved to put an end to her demonic reign. In the time since he'd last talked to her she'd assembled what was tantamount to a small army to patrol her streets and protect her. Still, it was Marcus who read insatiably and if there was anything he knew about it was the Art of War. And the art of war gave many ways to defeat an enemy but one of the most used was to simply cut off the head and watch the body

fall along with it. That was it. There was no other way. He would have to kill her. He was familiar with

killing and death. He had seen far too much of it in Italy. He had not only seen it he had taken part in

his fair share of the killing too. Many of the colored soldiers like his buddy Henry hadn't had a problem

with it. At first he thought it was because Henry had killed before but there were others like Henry who

killed at will and never looked back. He'd done his duty as well never shirking from the task at hand but

he'd never grown fond of taking another human beings life. And he wouldn't enjoy taking this woman's

life but it had to be done. Those soldiers in Italy had never done anything to

him and he had made light their existence so he would not have any qualms about the demise of this

woman who continued to bring heartbreak and tragedy to his life.

Getting out of the car a couple of blocks fro the office he walked briskly. The cold November air felt

good against his face. Walking up to the office a rather large man posing as a doorman stood there

fighting the cold. He relaxed somewhat as Marcus approached.

"Marcus. What's up my good man?"

"Not much. Not much good anyway. Where's Antwon?"

"Just ran down to the bodega to grab us a couple of coffees."

"Alright. When he gets back I want you to meet me at Sherman's. Call Mayweather and Mr. Jenner and

ask them to meet us there as well. Tell them it's a matter of dire importance."

"Gotcha boss."

An hour later the four men regrouped at an inconspicuous bar in the Bronx.

"I hope when tonight is over we can say this is our first and last mission. To be perfectly honest with you when I was discharged from Uncle Sam's War I thought that would be my last physical altercation. But then I never thought that I'd come back to Colored folks beating and stealing from each other."

"I don't know why. They was doing it when you left," he laughed along with the rest of the table.

"Don't know why. I guess I was just naive. I figured things would be different somehow changed for the better. I thought that's what we was over there fighting for a better world. Didn't think I was over there to make every place better but at home but it still say Colored when I go out to get something to eat."

"I hear you Marcus and speaking of eating the old lady just called to see where I am so what's up."

"I was just saying that I was hoping for better when I arrived home but nothing's changed much for the Negro at home. What I didn't expect was that now we have Colored folk exploiting each other. And we have them in our own community. There is a Negro woman who lives among us who is a chief culprit in this abuse. She has built a small army of volunteers n not to protect our interests but her own. I have been told that they are now involved in extortion, shake downs, you name it."

"They were supposed to protect the community," Mayweather said.

"That's what they were supposed to do but I have eyewitness testimony that an elite faction, an armed segment of her Christian Community Watch just beat up three young men. She is also responsible for the burning of a Colored business right here in Harlem. She must be stopped. Messages have been sent. She has ignored them. Do you recall the racists officers who spent their days denigrating and degrading Colored troops. When roll was called in the morning they would have mysteriously deserted in the night. Headquarters would write it off as Missing In Action but we knew better. They say close

to fifty percent of our troops go missing or are killed due to friendly fire and that's exactly the way I want this one to look."

"But this is a Colored woman Marcus."

"How old is Tyreke now Mayweather?"

The question brought a broad smile from Mayweather.

"He's two. Why you ask?"

"That's your first born and your heart and soul God forgive anything ever to happen to them but should someone inflict harm on Tyreke what would be your response?"

"I'd probably kill 'em."

"And would it make any difference if it were a man or a woman?"

"No."

"Then why would it make a difference now?"

When no one said anything Marcus spoke to the men just as he had overseas when they were about to go out on a mission. They trusted him and as their platoon leader he'd never lead them wrong.

"What I need for you to do is police the area while I put an end to this. Tommorrow I am going in and take her out."

"You are aware that the Christian Community Watch provides security for that part of Edgecombe?" Man said.

"And that will be your job Man. I need you to set up surveillance and see how often they patrol that part of Edgecombe. I want to be in and out between their patrols. Most of the people that provide security for the Watch are good, decent hard-working people so I don't want them hurt or endangered. I don't want any confrontation. If there is there instructions are to call in the heavy artillery and from what I understand they are heavily armed and will kill at will. So. our actions must be clandestine. Is that understood? Mayweather and I will be the only ones to go in. I need you two to provide surveillance and act as look outs."

I kept telling myself that 'it could be worse' but I wasn't sure.

A day later we met again. I'd served with them in uncle Sam's War and had to rely on them for my life on more than one occasion. And here we were once again confronted with our latest battle.

At nine forty-five we pulled up in front of Kathryn's building. We had an half an hour between Watch patrols and when the coast was clear Man and Mayweather took to the fire escape and entered the third floor window.

A few minutes later Mayweather opened the front door.

"What's up?"

"It's all good. She's here. Man has her bound and gagged in an upstairs bedroom. She's a feisty little thing. It took two of us just to tie her up. I feel sorry for her man but

Lord knows I'd have to leave home for that. She's one fine lookin' sister," Mayweather chuckled.

The sentiment was the same when I got inside with Man expressing almost the same words as Mayweather .

"Damn shame you have to do away with her son. She's one beautiful specimen. Any chance I can rehab her into being a productive citizen."

"No. Sorry This one's too far gone. She's hopeless," I laughed. "I'm sure you've heard that everything that looks good isn't good for you."

We were all masked but it really didn't matter. She was a dead woman.

"What the fuck is this all about?" Kathryn screamed as soon as the gag was removed.

"Think back Kathryn. Think back on all the lives that you've impacted and helped to ruin. And you posing as a Christian to do the devil's work. Cheating, stealing and lying to the poor and ignorant to fill your own pockets has never been part of Christ's teachings. Greed is not in Christ's teaching. It must end today. It has to end today," I shouted.

"Marcus? I'd know your voice anywhere. Now take off that silly mask and tell me what this is really all about it."

There was so much noise and confusion that none of us heard the big man until it was too late. Shots were fired. I could feel the hot lead as it burned its way into the calf of my leg and then pass out the other side, I hit the floor hard and heard Kathryn's shouts.

"Hank. Is that you? Kill these motherfuckers. Kill 'em and i will be ever indebted to you."

"Man. Mayweaher. Is that you?

"Take off your masks," The voice demanded.

"Doc, Mayweather, "The man acknowledged.

Me. Well, I'd know that voice anywhere.

"Henry Lucious," I yelled.

"Yeah. It's me. Marcus. I'll be damned if I'm not still saving your ass.

"Hank. You know this man? "Kathryn screamed.

"Kill the bastard hank."

"Kill him? Hank screamed back. "You're asking me to kill my friend you sheisty slut You don'tcMar even remember me do you? I guess not. Me and Marcus rented a roach infested flat from you a few years back before the war. I was crazy about you but I was poor and ignorant then and you couldn't see fit to give me time of the day. Ring a bell? And from what I understand you're still up to your old trucks. I imagine that's why my old friend Marcus has come to visit. From what I understand from Jennifer and her brothers you stole from her as well then lied and used me to beat these poor boys."

"Poor boys? Those niggas robbed me. Same thing these niggas are tryin' to do."

Henry lucious laughed.

"I spent years with these men overseas and I know them. These are good men. Men with families ansd I can vouch for everyone here. That is I can vouch for everyone except you."

"Sweetheart. Are you trying to tell me that you believe these losers over me?"

"Yes, that is exactly what I'm saying. My interests are for the retirement of negroes. Your interests are for the upliftment of Kathryn and no one else. We do not need people you if we are to build a nation. Mayweather there are two large duffel bags the in office downstairs. Take one and fill it with anything you consider of value. That's for those two boys you claimed beat and burglarred you. Check her pocketbook and the safe. Matter of fact, take the entire safe and load it into the black packard parked out front. Put it in the duffel bag as well."

"Be careful Henry the community watch is due about now," Marcus said a big small covered his face.

"No worries Marcus, I gave them another block to canvas."

"Always thinking Henry."

"Have to be."

"You'll never get away with this Hank. Once the word gets out you'll be ruined."

"And who's to say the word will get out. The only word that's going to get out is the one the tabloids run about how a jealous church wife did away with you for messing with her husband and how you commanded the largest prostitution ring in Harlem under the guise of the church. That's the way the tabloids will read."

"Let me tell you one thing you may not be aware of Mr. Whitted. I've been a member of the Breath of Life Church in Christ for close to twenty years. Now who do you think they're going to believe?"

About that time Mayweather and Doc walked in.

"You ready? The car's loaded. Just waiting on you boss."

"Yes. I do believe we're ready. You might want to go wait in the car. You don't want to be a witness to this."

 Once the men were gone Marcus unrolled the heavy plastic tarp before duct taping the woman's mouth once more despite her protests.

"You have any final words?" Marcus asked the gagged woman while Hank took the silencer from his pants pocket and screwed it to the tip of the barrel. The woman seeing the gun began ranting and raving but her words were muffled in lieu of the gag.

"I think she's trying to say she's sorry for all of the lives she's help to ruin."

"The Lord is a merciful and forgiving God. Well, let's hope so for your sake anyway," Hank said before emptying the little .22 to the back of her head.

"It could be worse you know."

"I don't see how."

CPSIA information can be obtained
at www.ICGtesting.com
Printed in the USA
LVOW09s1745140917

548744LV00007B/412/P

9 781542 551304